One for s
Three for a
Five for silver, six for gold,
Seven for a secret never to be told,
Eight for a wish, nine for a kiss . . .

for a 7 Secret

Jenny Oldfield

Hodder
Children's
Books

a division of Hodder Headline

First published in Great Britain in 2000
by Hodder Children's Books

10 9 8 7 6 5 4 3 2 1

Visit Jenny Oldfield's website at
www.testware.co.uk/jenny.oldfield

A Catalogue record for this book is available from
the British Library

ISBN 0 340 77862 8

Typeset by Avon Dataset Ltd, Bidford-on-Avon, Warks

Printed and bound in Great Britain by
Clays Ltd, St Ives plc

Hodder Children's Books
a division of Hodder Headline
338 Euston Road
London NW1 3BH

1

I'm stretched out on the grass in Fortune Park, enjoying the sun.

'Kate, you wanna end up with skin cancer?' Connie asks.

Thanks, Con. I deliberately ignore the advice to join her in the shade, where she and Zoey are deep into the fashion pages of *Cosmo*. Well, I hold out for thirty seconds, just to prove I have a mind of my own. Then I move out of the sun.

I mean, I take all that ozone stuff seriously.

Unlike Carter and Ziggy. Those two airheads are stripped to the waist, cantering around the park with a basketball. Zig's rehearsing moves for the up and coming inter-school tournament.

One-two-three steps – bounce-bounce – dribble-dribble – sprint – pivot – pass.

Carter makes a neat catch and imitates Zig's style. I gotta admit he's not exactly in Ziggy's league. But then again, his bare torso does look pretty neat.

1

Smooth and tanned. Kind of rippling.

Connie looks up from her mag. 'I guess you don't want me to issue the ozone warning to the boys over there?' she asks me slyly.

Zoey finds this real funny. 'Here, Kate. Take my sunblock, why don't you? You could offer to apply it liberally to Joey's back!'

She tosses me a plastic bottle which I make a point of refusing to catch. The top pops off as it lands on *Cosmo* and the oily contents splurge over the Face of the Millennium.

'Yuck!' Connie protests. She wipes the page clean with the edge of her hand, then slops the excess cream on to my thigh.

Bounce-bounce – run-run-run. As I hastily rub in the sunblock, the boys are heading our way. They pretend the basket is nailed to the tree above our heads. Carter passes the ball to Zig. All six-feet-two of Ziggy soars into the air, arm outstretched. He takes a shot at the imaginary goal. The ball hits the trunk and smacks down on to Con's fashion pages.

'Jeez!' she groans, smoothing out the mess.

This is just to give you a flavour of how we spend our summer. Zoey and Zig. Me and Joey. Connie.

Life's a beach. Or, at least, a green park in the middle of a pretty neat city.

Nothing to mess up our heads, except the truly mind-blowing fact that something that feels as nice and relaxing on your body as the sun's rays can actually kill you.

'So you see it's not cool to fry your skin,' Connie was explaining to Zig, now that the boys had flopped down beside us.

Connie herself stays a delicate shade of white, whatever the weather. The day before we met up in Fortune Park, she had changed her hair colour from jet black to straw blonde and we were currently trying to recognise her as the same girl. She still wore the nose ring and the belly button stud, and moaned about the mess we'd made of her glossy pages, so I guess she hadn't switched personalities along with her appearance.

'Uh,' was Zig's response to Connie's lecture on the ozone layer. He snuggled up beside Zoey like some outsize puppy dog. She ran a smug hand through his hair, then gave him an adoring peck on the cheek.

Now, if you ask me, that's not cool either.

I keep a decent physical distance from Joey in public. In private too, for that matter. Like, we don't move on in terms of a personal relationship, though he's helped me out of bad trouble in the past, and vice versa.

Don't ask me why. It's just how it is.

I was still admiring his torso when Connie held up the smudged pages of her magazine.

'A bright orange tan isn't cool health-wise,' she insisted, 'and it's not cool in image terms either. Forget Pamela Anderson. Think Elke, the Face of the Millennium!'

'Huh?' Catching sight of a picture of an attractive woman in very few clothes, Ziggy rolled away from Zoey towards Con. 'Elke who?' he asked, taking the mag from her with new interest.

'Elke nothing. Just Elke,' Zoey explained. Like the fact that the latest supermodel to appear and shine bright in the fashion firmament didn't have a surname wasn't worth Zig bothering his pretty head about. 'She's just some anorexic freak they're making a big thing out of at the moment. Tomorrow she'll be history.'

I could see Zig didn't agree. Neither did Carter. They bothed pored over the smudged photo with enthusiasm.

'The point is, no one would say Elke has spent much time under a sun lamp,' Con went on.

4

Zig and Joey noted her white skin and how much of it she was showing to the photographer. I was more interested in Joey's reactions than in the supermodel, but I did cast a glance at the picture: tall blonde girl, arms and legs like sticks. A little bruised and damaged looking, with sad, dark eyes. And yeah, she was pale.

'D'you see how much this swimsuit costs!' Zoey stabbed her finger at the print under the photo, unsuccessfully trying to divert Zig's attention.

'I wouldn't call her the Face of the Millennium exactly.' Connie forgot the ozone kick and she too grew critical. 'Her mouth's kinda wide, don't you think?'

'Like Julia Roberts.' Zoey extended the analysis.

'Never mind her face. What about the rest?' Carter passed what was for him an unworthy remark. He never says personal stuff like this; he usually just sits there and looks cynical.

'What d'you mean, what about the rest?' I jumped in with both big feet. I mean, it looked like I was jealous of a picture, for God's sake!

He flicked me a look. Said nothing.

'Hey!' Con crowed. 'Do I detect a *frisson*?'

'Shut up, Connie,' Carter and I both said.

'Anyway, I'm about to meet this world-famous supermodel, if anyone's interested,' I said casually.

I wasn't making it up, honest. My dad, Sean Brennan, produces TV programmes for Angel Christian, if you didn't know. And I get invites to the studio. No big deal. So I wasn't expecting the explosion of interest.

'How come?'

'When?'

'Where?'

'Wow!'

'At the Angelworks studio, tomorrow as a matter of fact,' I told them. 'Angel's doing a documentary on supermodels. Since Elke's the biggest name in modelling at the moment, she gets to be on the show.'

'Can we come along?' Zoey wanted to know.

Con and Zig joined in.

'Yeah, that'd be cool.'

'Wow, you mean we'd get to meet her in the flesh?'

I noticed Carter still said nothing. He was staring at the grass.

'Sure. Why don't you all show up at the studio at eleven a.m.?' This was to prove to Carter specifically that he could drool close-up and for real over any supermodel he liked and it wouldn't bother me one bit.

6

Connie snatched back the magazine from Ziggy. Time to split.

'Cool,' everyone said as we sloped off on our different ways.

Bounce-bounce – swerve – run. Zig headed for his coaching session at the leisure centre across the park.

Connie and Zoey decided on some serious shopping to get ready for the studio visit. Cosmetics were the key, they said. When you met a supermodel, it was important to get your eyeliner and blusher right.

'How about you?' Joey asked me quietly. We were the only two left in the shade of the tree.

I shrugged and lied. 'I'm meeting my dad,' I told him. Privately I was thinking, *Jeez, I must be crazy.*

I thought a lot about Elke as I said goodbye to Carter and left the park. Whatever Zoey and Connie said about her mouth, there was still that body, those eyes.

No doubt about it, Elke was stunning. And, yes, I had just fixed up for Carter to meet the biggest babe in the entire world.

'Did the hair stylist finish with Elke yet?' A studio runner did her job. She ran across the studio.

'Suzi, ask the agent if Elke agrees to still pictures being used on billboards to advertise the show.' My

7

dad, Sean Brennan, intercepted the runner to establish an important point.

'Elke's mother is her agent,' Suzi told him. 'She's the woman in the corner, talking to Angel.'

'So ask her,' Dad insisted. He had a pair of headphones slung around his neck and he looked uptight. I recognise this when others wouldn't. It's something about the way he juts out his chin and slows down his voice, meaning, 'Don't screw up, or else!' Hard to pin this down, until you remember that my dad is normally the gentlest, most laid back guy you could hope to meet. He's kinda shy too, which makes him tuck in his chin and look up at you from under his dark eyebrows with a half-smile. That's when he's not uptight, like he was now.

Suzi the runner plucked up courage to approach Angel's corner. I watched her clasp her clip-board to her chest and hover, waiting for a gap in the conversation.

Meanwhile, every other gaze in the studio had to be on the door which Elke was expected to walk through any minute now. Connie and Zoey, Ziggy and Carter; their eyes were all glued on that space.

And all the time, Angel Christian talked to Annika Svennivig.

Angel equals major media star. Equals ego to match. She owns her own production company and lives in a different stratosphere to the rest of us. Her wish is our command.

Don't get me wrong; I like Angel. Not a lot, but more than you might expect. She's better when her husband, Tommy Jett, is around, because we all love Tommy for the ex-alcoholic and 'B' list actor he is. And he genuinely loves his wife, and that's cosy, so she gets to act more like a normal human being when he's on the scene. Right now, though, Tommy's working in Europe, playing the bad guy in a costume drama set in Venice.

Which is why, in a roundabout way, my dad is uptight. Angel is lousy to everyone when Tommy works away.

So to see Mrs Svennivig getting the lion's share of the conversation with Angel was a little surprising.

You have to picture them. Angel is small, with glossy dark brown hair which is cut in a feathery style to give maximum lift and movement. She wears high heels and the best lilac, lime green or sunburst yellow tailored suits that money can buy. Today is forget-me-not blue.

Mrs Svennivig is tall and blonde like her daughter. She has that Scandinavian Ice-Queen look. Clear grey eyes, high cheekbones, no expression on her face. And you would call her dress understated beside Angel: tasteful taupe (what you and I would call dark beige), with designer gold necklace and matching earrings. She wears her long hair swept back and twisted up, with more gold clips to keep it in place.

Enough of the fashion details. Tension was mounting as the technicians, runners, assistant producers and the rest waited for Elke to make her entrance. And in Angel's corner, an argument was developing.

'It's not in the contract,' Annika Svennivig said, loud enough to draw our attention. She was obviously contradicting something that Angel had just said.

'Yeah, but we don't spell out in the written contract every line of questioning we might care to follow,' Angel pointed out. She obviously thought she was being patient and considerate to the visitor, but the use of the royal 'we' gave her away.

'This could hit the fan!' my dad muttered to me, chin jutting out, as he strode over coils of cable nearby.

'Elke doesn't take questions about her family circumstances,' Annika insisted. She was five inches taller than Angel, and used this to her advantage by tilting her head in a way that a school principal might use to make a student feel they'd best not argue.

'But the focus of this documentary is on the life of the supermodels *away* from the camera lens.' Angel reminded the agent-mother that this much had been made perfectly clear from the start.

'Questions about family are always off-limits as far as Elke is concerned.' Annika didn't mind that by this time the whole studio was staring. 'We don't do that type of gutter journalism; people prying into our private lives. Oh, and one more thing: no questions about eating disorders, OK!'

Angel drew a deep breath. 'Wouldn't you say you're being a little overprotective here, Annika? Surely Elke can decide for herself how to handle the questions I might pose.'

'She's seventeen years old,' Mrs Svennivig countered. 'Do you call that old enough to be able to handle an interviewer of your experience, Ms Christian?'

The breath came out as a loud sigh. 'This is beginning to sound like you or your daughter may have something to hide, Mrs Svenn . . .' Angel paused to consult the front of her pre-prepared set of questions for the interview, '. . . Mrs Svennivig.'

'Erm, excuse me . . .' Runner Suzi, still hovering

with her clip-board, broke the freezing silence that developed. 'I need to know—'

'Not now, Suzi!' Angel snapped. She closed her eyes as if summoning her last shred of patience. 'Annika, it seems to me to be a question of trust,' she said, as steadily as she could.

But Annika shook her head. 'Not at all, Angel. Trust doesn't come into it. What matters is what's set out in the contract.'

I could feel myself staring and my mouth beginning to hang open. No way did anyone do this to Angel Christian. Dad was right about stuff hitting the fan.

There was a second long silence, which Suzi foolishly tried to fill. 'Erm, about still pictures for publicity purposes—'

'Cut it out!' Angel snarled.

Suzi recoiled as if she'd been bitten by a dog. I didn't rate her chances of survival in the Angelworks studio above one in a thousand unless a diversion occurred.

Which it did. Because Elke timed her entrance for right that moment.

I mean, she doesn't just come into a room. She enters. It's like she carries a personal spotlight with her wherever she goes. *Zoom!* All heads swing round.

There's this creature standing in the doorway,

so thin you wonder how she can stand.

('I don't think it's politically correct to look that way!' Connie muttered in my ear. 'I mean, how many kids go on crash diets after they've seen pictures of her? There are millions of wannabe supermodels around the place, all surviving on a lettuce leaf and a cup of lemon juice per day!')

There's this dazzling effect. You can't tear your attention away. Long, golden hair, the slash of a red mouth slightly turned down at the corners, skin pulled taut over high cheeks, and moody, heavy-lidded, huge dark eyes.

('Wow!' Ziggy and Zoey whispered.)

Elke wore sizzling, shiny, strapless, skin-tight red. And strappy, tottery shoes. Like it wasn't hot enough in the studio already.

(Carter said nothing. I felt him catch his breath though.)

Great idea, Kate! I told myself. I dress casual and sporty, judge it so that no heads turn on the street.

'Honey!' Annika Svennivig said, breaking away from her tête-à-tête with Angel. 'You look fabulous, as always. But we do have a small problem . . .'

'Jeez, jeez, jeez, she's gonna pull the interview!' Dad rushed by, muttering under his breath.

Annika took her daughter by a thin arm and led her into another, more private corner. All heads did turn. But Mrs S was expert in the art of talking low as well as loud and clear. We saw Elke listen and occasionally nod her head.

'She's not great,' a quiet voice said in my ear.

I turned sharply. 'Yeah, Carter – put that in writing, will you?'

'She's not,' he insisted.

'Yeah, yeah, Joey. I know you're an adoring fan, so there's no need to try to make the rest of us girls feel better.' I wondered if he was winding me up again.

'Truth. She doesn't look real. She's like she is in the magazine: kinda plastic.'

Maybe. But she had legs to die for. And curves in the right place. That is, in the only place a girl wants to have curves.

'Her face doesn't move,' Joey pointed out. 'You can't see what she's thinking.'

Only Joey Carter could look at the world's top supermodel – the Face and the Body – and wonder what went on in her head. It made me want to laugh and hug him. But I held back.

Annika had finished talking to her daughter by this

time and Angel was sending my dad across the studio to renegotiate.

'Except that she looks like she wishes she was some place else,' Carter went on.

Sweet! I listened and watched the unravelling situation.

'Like, I never saw anybody look more unhappy.' Joey shrugged then frowned.

'So would you if you only ate rabbit food!' Connie hissed.

'Sssh!' Zoey wanted to find out if the interview was on or off.

'. . . We'll do it your way,' Dad was telling dragon-mother and the Face. 'No references to personal matters. Only to the professional aspects of the job, OK?'

This was unbelievable. Angel had caved in. I guess even she must have realised that a documentary on top supermodels couldn't go ahead without including *the* top supermodel. She'd told my dad to concede to Annika's conditions.

You could hear the awed gasps amongst the technicians and runners.

Mrs Svennivig greeted the news with a cold, wary nod, then turned to her daughter. 'You hear that, honey? They'll stick to the script.'

We all noticed that Elke didn't react. Her beautiful face was like a mask.

And it made me wonder, as they sat her down and clipped on the mike, fussed with her hair, re-angled the lights. I mean, was Carter right? Was the Face of the Millennium a picture of misery beneath the mask? Behind the crimson lips and the kohl-darkened eyes?

2

I'd rather be at the ball game.

This was what I told myself when some hack journo stepped on my trainers in the crush to get near the superstars.

Ziggy was playing for the inter-state under-eighteens. Major problem. Do I go to yell and cheer for my best buddy, or do I accept Kate's invite to the book launch? Maybe it doesn't sound much, but to me it was a big deal.

I ended up at the launch.

Mucho complexo. The look on Zig's face told me I'd let him down. Even when I confided that if it had been up to me personally, I'd rather be at the game any day.

The reason I was being jabbed in the guts by photographers and stepped on ten times a minute was Kate. I mean, if she asked me to walk through fire I'd do it.

'Carter, how about you and me using these?' She'd casually thrown a couple of tickets in my direction. We'd been bumming around in the basement at my place, listening to the band jamming.

By 'the band', I mean Synergie, my sister Marcie's gold disc winning outfit. I'm not name-dropping. It just so happens that Marcie made it big time. Anyhow, it's not important.

I'd glanced at the passes. They would get us in to the Angelworks party at the biggest bookstore in town. The whole deal had been set up to launch the book on supermodels that was being published on the back of Angel's TV documentary on the subject. They would all be there: Gemini Jones, Tanya Childe, Belinda Mason, and of course Elke.

Zoey and Connie, who'd been in my basement at the time, said the passes were like gold dust. Everyone wanted to rub shoulders with the supermodels. Or get their feet trodden on. Whatever.

So I said yes because the look on Kate's face would have been worse than Ziggy's if I'd said no. So I was here and getting crushed to death.

And I guess it was cool from a fly-on-the-wall point of view. It made me ask questions. Like, how come these journos worked themselves into a frenzy for a cheap photo of a bunch of girls in glittery party dresses, or for one exclusive, airhead comment?

'Big bucks at stake,' Kate told me. She was dodging the jabbing elbows and flashing lights at the time. 'One good picture of these four women partying together would put a photographer's kids through school!'

'OK.' I admitted this was pretty obvious when you thought about it. A magazine editor would pay one of these freelance guys thousands of dollars; more if the lens had caught the models off-guard and doing something they oughtn't. A hundred thousand for an unintentional flash of private flesh, for instance. 'But how come the world wants the picture in the first place?'

More flashes. Of Gemini hugging Tanya and Elke talking quietly to her mom.

No reply from Kate.

I guess I'd lost her attention. Maybe because Angel Christian was standing up to make a speech, and when God talks, the world of Angelworks listens.

Actually, considering the way Angel and Annika had argued at the studio two weeks back, I was pretty amazed that the launch party had come together the way it had. But as Kate would say, 'Big bucks talk.'

The interview had gone something like this:

Angel Is it true what we read, Elke, that you have this

	big thing about being shy about your body?
Elke	Yes, that's true. When I was a kid in high school I spent a whole lot of time trying to cover myself up with three shirts or with baggy sweaters. That kind of stuff. I didn't like the way I looked. (Audience laughter)
Angel	That's kind of ironic, don't you think? (Camera on the strapless, shiny red number that Elke is wearing. Elke doesn't crack a smile.)
Elke	Most kids feel that way.
Angel	Yeah, but most kids don't go on to become possibly the most photographed face in the US.
Elke	But that happened by accident, you know. I mean, an inhibited kid like me doesn't set out to be a fashion model.
Angel	So, how come?
Elke	Well, everybody knows the story, don't they? It was all down to my mom sending in my picture to a competition in magazine. I didn't know she'd done it. The first I heard was when I won first prize. I had to fly to New York for a big makeover: before and after shots, that kind of stuff.
Angel	And the rest, as they say, is history. That was three years back, when you were fourteen years old; a skinny kid still seeing the orthodontist. Proud

	momma pushes her daughter in to big-time fashion modelling.
Elke	(cutting in fast) My mom didn't have to push.
Angel	(smoothing things over) Sure. No one wants to take away from what you've achieved, Elke. The hard work, the professionalism. But at fourteen, fifteen – didn't you sometimes just want to chill out with the rest of the kids?

(There's a complication here. Kate later told me that Angel herself had been the victim of a pushy mother. So I guess that's where this question came from.)

Elke	(her face glazing over with a stubborn look) You're making it sound all wrong. Listen, modelling is my life and I like it that way. Sure, I was inhibited when I first started up. I felt negative about myself. But I soon learned that for some reason I looked good in pictures; something about the way I react to the camera. Don't ask me. Good bone structure, good skin tone, small features that make-up artists can work with . . .
Angel	You don't sound happy about this. You talk about yourself from a distance, as if you're an object—

(Annika Svennivig walks on set. She's not miked

21

up so we don't hear what she's saying, but it's definitely not friendly. The director yells 'Cut!' That's it. End of interview. Kate's dad steps in to hustle the small audience out of the studio.)

After the argument, I guess Annika had grabbed back editorial control of the small amount of studio footage they'd shot. It must have left Kate's dad only snippets to work with, but enough to make the programme hang together. They'd used loads of stuff showing Elke on the catwalks of Paris, Milan, Tokyo, New York. The professional angle, which is what Annika had been pitching for all along. The glitz and the glamour.

And then there were the behind-the-scenes interviews with Gemini, Tanya and Belinda. Luckily these girls had agents who weren't Rottweilers like Mrs Svennivig.

They'd even scrambled a book together in record time, ready for the screening of the documentary on network TV. A glossy, full-colour, coffee-table number going under the title of 'Angel on Supermodels'. Snappy, huh? It follows on from 'Angel on Politicians', 'Angel on Movie Stars', get it? They must sell pretty well, otherwise she wouldn't go through the hassle.

Like this launch party. I looked around and saw that I wasn't the only one who wished I was some place else.

Sean Brennan for instance. What was a nice guy like him doing in a dive like this? When I say dive, I mean there were people here who would sell a picture of their grandmother taking a shower, if it happened to be the right grandmother.

And Kate. She didn't look too impressed by the hair lacquer and lip gloss either. She was cool in a figure-hugging grey top and silky light grey trousers with splits up the side. Her face was beautiful without a slick of make-up. Her dark hair was piled on top of her head as if that was the way it had just landed and been pinned into place.

For that matter, I counted Elke among the people not enjoying the occasion. So, she never looks happy; I knew that already. Her fashion pictures specialise in mean and moody. Grainy black and white, selling leather jackets with loads of zippers against an urban setting. Not Bermuda shorts on a palm-fringed beach. And her facial muscles probably wouldn't remember how to smile even if her brain tried to send the message. Which it obviously didn't.

'Back off!' the goons were telling the crowd.

Things were getting a little out of hand, even though entry was by ticket only. Two photographers had pushed through to the place where the supermodels sat signing copies of the book. One had shoved her camera right into Elke's face.

Elke looked unnerved, like she was about to cry or something. That's why I say she wasn't enjoying the attention.

Momma Svennivig moved in as the two men in black re-established a safe distance between the journos and their subjects.

'Elke is tired,' she announced to the hundreds of eager customers patient enough to wait in line. 'She can only sign fifty more copies; after that, I'm afraid we must leave!' Annika had got it sussed: if you create a limited supply, you automatically increase demand. That's the Joey Carter Third Rule for Living.

'Aww!' people protested; those who were way back beyond fifty in the line. Little wannabe models in pencil skirts and high heels, professional celebrity oglers in shapeless beige cotton anoraks. 'Hey, Elke; you gotta write in my book. I already paid the store twenty dollars for it!'

'Sorry!' Mrs Svennivig stood firm and counted, while Elke kept her head down and went on signing.

'She hates every second!' Kate had noticed the same thing as me. That the smiles on Gemini, Tanya and Belinda's faces were a genuine mixture of glossy pride and smugness, whereas it was taking Elke all her time to hold it together.

Meanwhile, beyond the living security barrier of suits, the press hassle continued.

'Elke, look up, will ya!'

'Turn around, face this way!'

'C'mon, be nice, Elke. Just one big pout for the camera!'

Annika counted thirty. She was concentrating on the orderly though by now grumbling line. Meanwhile, in the press pack where Kate and I stood, more ribs were jabbed, more feet trampled.

I caught sight of Angel, in the background for once, talking urgently to Kate's dad. She was pointing towards a guy in the mob of press people who seemed to be making more trouble than the rest. This guy didn't even have a camera, but he was practically climbing over shoulders to get to the front.

I saw Sean mark the guy, then nod. He spoke into a cell-phone that brought more suits in from outside the door, maybe six or seven security guards with broad shoulders and brutal haircuts.

'Thanks, Elke. I just adore your look!' a female fan enthused as the top model slid her signed book across the table for her to take up. 'I wanted to know, what shampoo d'you use?'

Elke named a brand and sent sales of the product rocketing. 'Because I'm worth it!'

OK, so I watch the adverts on TV. Sad.

Annika had her back turned to us, still busily sorting out the line. The guy pressed on, regardless of whose camera he nearly ripped out of their hands in his effort to get to the front.

'Man!' an ex-hippy photographer wearing his long grey hair in a thin ponytail complained. 'Like, what's the deal here? We're all in this together, yeah!'

The guy didn't seem to hear. And by now the reinforcement heavies were shoving through from behind. Miraculously the sea of bodies had begun to part and they were making good progress towards the super-determined, crazy-looking guy.

I say crazy because of the expression on his face. It made me step automatically to one side as he pushed past. And I grabbed Kate to clear her out of his track. The look was one of blind determination, like he didn't see and it didn't matter who he had to push to one side or crawl over.

'Man, he's out of his head on something!' the ex-hippy muttered, having caught the same look.

I could see what he meant, though to me it didn't seem to have to do with drugs. The guy was too focused for that. But hey, what did I know?

Only that the security guys were on red alert, and that Elke was definitely the supermodel that the guy was aiming at.

By this time he'd begun to call out her name, but his voice was mostly drowned out by the buzz going on around the tables stacked with pristine copies of 'Angel on Supermodels'.

It was only when he broke through to the front of the press pack that people in general realised something was wrong. He launched himself across the small space and stumbled against the nearest table, occupied by Gemini. She screamed, jumped to her feet and the whole place fell silent.

Annika Svennivig turned and registered the situation. It was obvious to me that she recognised the tall, thin guy with the shadowy face and the unreadable eyes. Like it was instant; the shock and the attempt to screen her daughter from him.

All the models stood up and huddled in a tight bunch, with Annika standing guard, arms stretched wide, shielding Elke.

Suits piled in from every direction. They outnumbered the enemy about twenty to one.

The word 'Stalker!' passed Kate's lips and a hundred

others. Otherwise, we all stood in stunned, helpless silence.

Some guy obsessed with the haughty beauty of an untouchable photographic image. A crazy man who, because he had Elke's semi-nude pictures pinned to his wall, thought he owned a piece of her. I understand this stuff when I hear it in the news headlines. And I guess I recognise obsession too.

But only for a girl that you talk to every day at school and bum around in a basement with. One whose sense of humour is the same as yours, whose qualities you get to know over a period of time. And, to be frank, whose body you lust after in close but painful silence. You all know who I mean.

This weird celebrity worship is beyond me, man.

The security guards were taking no chances. Guns came out of shoulder holsters. Everyone in the room froze and looked for the nearest cover.

'Elke!' the guy called out as four heavies threw themselves on top of him.

She caught a glimpse of him before he disappeared, shot a wild glance at her mother, let herself sag against Gemini, hide her face and start to cry.

Anyone who suffered from epilepsy should not have been in that bookstore at that moment in time. The way the cameras flashed in a blinding, jerky frenzy made even me feel queasy. With the potential attacker squashed flat by guards and Elke falling apart before their eyes, this was too good a chance for the lean and hungry photographers to miss.

Bonus: things got so rough again that Kate was knocked sideways and into my arms. I got to stand her back upright and help brush her down.

'Elke!' the invisible guy cried out with real desperation. 'Get your hands off of me, you dumb gorillas! I have a right to speak to my own daughter, don't I?'

I heard this and so did Kate. I don't know how many others. It cast a whole new light on things.

We watched Annika rescue Elke from Gemini and surround themselves with guards. She demanded quick and speedy exit from the store.

Elke went along with this without resisting, still hiding her face and putting up one hand to stave off the crowd. Within seconds they were out on the sidewalk, then they were instantly whisked away in a waiting limo. Corny but true.

Not so lucky the buried assailant. When the guards finally hauled him to his feet, there was blood pouring from his nose. But still his only concern was to get to Elke. He went crazy trying to wrestle off four big guys to follow her to the door.

No way. They pinned his arms back and put a forearm across his throat. He wasn't going anywhere.

Except in the company of the suits.

We all watched them drag him out the back way, through a door marked 'Staff Only'.

Imagine an underground storage bay, the smell of diesel, a dimly-lit concrete ramp and the sound of boots going in heavy.

Meanwhile, back in the store where Kate and I stood amazed, Angel was getting the three remaining supermodels back in order. 'Sit!' she told them. 'The guy's being dealt with. End of story!'

Belinda, Tanya and Gemini straightened their skirts and checked their mirrors to see that they were fit to resume business. The customers who'd been waiting in line for Elke made the best of it and melted into the lines for the other three girls.

'Did you hear what he said?' Kate hissed at me. She was the first to find her voice.

I nodded.

'That guy was Elke's father!'

'I know.'

Which raised many questions.

And maybe explained Annika's no-prying-into-private-life rule. Plus, it gave you a clue as to why Elke wasn't a

30

happy superstar. Family skeleton rattling loudly.

'OK, gentlemen!' Angel announced briskly, ignoring the fact that four models were unaccountably reduced to three. 'Excitement over. We're back open for business!'

3

It made me glad to be Ms Average. I mean, seriously, who would choose to turn themselves into media fodder like those fashion models from last night? OK, there's the money and the ego trip; everyone telling you how beautiful you are, your face on the front cover of every major magazine. But they steal your life, believe me.

For example, if I was Elke or Gemini, would I be able to stroll over from my place on a sunny Saturday afternoon in mid-July to meet up in Joey's basement with the rest of the gang? Or fool around with Carter's kid sister, Fern, trying to teach her a couple of chords on Ocean's guitar?

Actually, Fern is Carter's half-sister/step-sister. What do you call it when the family adopts a kid? Anyhow, she was adopted by Mr and Mrs Carter, and my heart warms up just at the sight of her. She's small and skinny with jet-black hair and big brown eyes; Mexican looking. And she has a hearing problem. I just want to hug her every time.

So Fern was listening hard to the noise made by the guitar and nodding like crazy when she managed to pick up a note. We were all smiling and laughing and treating her like a little princess because she had a lot of lost years to catch up on to make her equal with other kids.

The Carters brought her into their family after her drug-addict mother had been shot dead in the street. That's how the Carter parents are: no money but big-hearted. Marcie's paying for Fern to see the best audiologist in town, and they're planning surgery soon to recover sixty per cent of normal hearing. We're gonna have the biggest party.

'So tell me again!' I'd been working with Fern on a G chord for ten minutes when Connie hassled Joey to repeat his account of the book launch. She'd already read the morning paper and seen the pictures of a guy with a bloody nose exiting under armed escort. 'You're saying that this stalker was claiming to be Elke's dad?'

Carter nodded then beat out a drum roll. The basement exploded with sound. Fern looked up and grinned from ear to ear.

'So why wasn't that part about the father in the *Fortune City Times?*' Connie quizzed.

'I guess not too many people heard what he said. Or

else, they've got him down as some kind of nut.' Joey was obviously bored with the topic. He and Connie often had a personality clash; he was so laid back and she hassled at stuff. Like, she has this logical type brain and he's more intuitive.

'Maybe you got it wrong,' she persisted. 'Maybe he didn't mention the word "daughter".'

'He did,' I put in quietly. Fact.

Carter looked grateful to me for getting Con off his back.

Things moved on for a bit. Zig and Zoey sprawled in a corner, celebrating his victory in last night's ball game in their own intimate little way. Connie drifted to the keyboard and picked out a kindergarten tune.

I let Fern practise the chord and found myself working out the Elke and her father scenario.

Just suppose, a) the guy really is who he says he is. Which means, b) he's been prevented from seeing his daughter. Which makes me wonder, c) who by? And d) for what reason? Oh, and e) what is Elke's reaction to all this?

I know for sure how I'd feel if they tried to keep me away from my dad. I could give you an alphabetful of reasons why it would never happen. But suppose someone tried!

I felt so strongly about this, I voiced it out loud.

'I feel the same.' Con looked like a warrior woman at the very idea that she and her dad could ever be parted.

But Zoey disentangled herself from Ziggy and said that sadly some fathers didn't live up to expectations. 'Like mine,' she added. Then looked guilty at the betrayal.

It was OK; we all knew that Zoey had a bad scene with her dad. He'd left when she was five years old, taking her ten-year-old brother, Billy, along with him. The pattern was, he and Billy would show up every few months, borrow money from her mom, then disappear again.

'Yeah, but Zoey, it's not as if your dad's real crazy, or something; like this guy last night!'

I guess she meant it as some kind of comfort. Zoey's father might be a low-down louse, but he was no nutcase. We all found this hysterical.

When we stopped laughing, we did admit that if the guy last night had been telling the truth, Elke had one seriously weird situation to handle.

And that had been as far as we'd got.

A few more gags, a few more chords and drum rolls.

Hugs and a trip to the candy store for Fern. Then we all went home.

Nothing conclusive. In fact, the Elke affair was drifting to the edge of my consciousness until precisely eight p.m. that same evening, when there was firm pressure on our door buzzer at number 18 Constitution Square, and the world turned upside-down.

'Angel!' my dad and I both exclaimed. We recognised her buzzing style: '*Open this door immediately!*'

A visitation from Angel in person was not an everyday thing. Faxes, phone calls, e-mails; yeah. But a person-to-person conversation in our hallway happened maybe twice a year and it usually took hours of planning to get her there.

So I jumped up and began hiding a stack of crumpled newspapers and magazines under cushions while Dad went to the door. When he didn't show Angel in, as expected, it meant I had to go out into the hall.

I could see straightaway that it wasn't a social call. Angel had stepped inside the house, but the door was still open, one of her cars parked with two wheels on the sidewalk behind her. Her mood was uptight-but-I-can-handle-it and she was talking rapidly at my puzzled dad.

'So you get the picture?' she asked him as I cleared my throat ready to say hi.

'No. Run that by me one more time,' he urged.

Angel spied me and rushed to draw me across. 'Kate, honey, Sean is being awfully slow, so I have to explain this situation to you. Then I want you to give me a straight yes or no, OK?'

I nodded. You always nod when Angel shoots one of her 'OKs?' at you.

'So, this is it. I have Elke waiting in my car!'

I frowned and glanced out the door. Yeah, there was a figure huddled in the back seat.

'Do I bring her in? Or do I leave her at the mercy of some lunatic stalker who just tried to kill her mother?'

Whoa! My mouth dropped open. I grunted something that I couldn't expect anyone to understand.

'Katie?' Angel's patience had limits. She let us know she'd just reached them. 'Yes or no?'

'Yeah, bring her in!' I gasped, glancing at my dad to see that he agreed.

So Angel made a James Bond dash down our front stoop to the car. Opening the back door, she hustled her passenger out and back up the steps, taking exaggerated glances to left and right and checking the rooftops along our street.

What did she expect: spies, mobsters, hitmen lurking behind trees in the centre of the Square?

The second she got Elke in through the door and closed it tight, she switched from being 007 to big Italian momma. 'You poor little girl!' she cried. 'You're trembling all over! Here, dry your eyes. You're safe now. No nasty, horrible creep of a stalker knows you're here!'

It was time for my dad to step in. 'Hold it, Angel. You're telling us that the same guy who was at the launch yesterday just tried to kill Annika Svennivig? Is this a theory or is it fact?'

His boss withered him with a look. 'At this moment in time, Annika is lying unconscious in a hospital bed with possibly severe spinal injuries!'

Elke cried louder at this. My brain was still scrambled, so in my press-ganged role as comforter I was pretty lousy.

'The official version is she landed there through an accident at her hotel, but we know different!' Angel swept on. 'I mean; get real! How does a perfectly fit woman of forty fall down two flights of stairs?'

'And how come you're involved?' My dad was still trying to get his head around the present connection between Angel and the Svennivigs. He knew better than most that the two older women weren't exactly soul mates.

Angel arched her eyebrows. 'I happened to have my secretary telephone Annika just after it happened. Some contractual stuff, y'know. Elke came on the phone and told me about her mother's so-called accident. She sounded like she'd fallen apart, so of course I had my driver drive round to the hotel to bring her back to Heaven's Gate.'

Dad nodded slowly. Like me, he was having difficulty casting Angel as the Mother Teresa type. 'What's in it for her?' was the more useful question we should be asking.

Explanations out of the way, Angel began to look around. 'Who's gonna make coffee?' she said, staring directly at me. 'And which room is Elke gonna sleep in? Can you call the housekeeper to change the bed linen?'

While Dad explained to Angel that not everyone has a live-in housekeeper, I quietly took Elke through to the kitchen. 'You OK? I checked. Words do kind of let me down in a crisis.

Elke took a deep breath and made a big effort. She nodded without saying anything. When I handed her a mug of instant, black without sugar, she was still shaking from head to foot.

'You're *not* OK?' I conceded.

She shook her head and made the tears spill over the rim of her dark eyes, and trickle between those gorgeous curved lashes.

'You wanna tell me?' I wanted her version, not Angel's wild guesses.

'I can't . . .' she stammered.

Weird how tears break down barriers. Up till this point I'd been regarding Elke as an alien species. Like Joey said, kind of made of plastic. But these tears were for real. And the trembling, crooked mouth, the blotched cheeks and the shuddering, thin shoulders.

'Sure you can,' I whispered, moving in, about to put an arm around her.

'. . . So, Elke, honey, you have a nice room at the back of the house. Sean just showed me where you'll sleep.' Angel bustled back in, full of plans. 'He and Katie will block all phone calls. They'll fix it so that the hospital rings this number with news about your mom.'

I pulled my dad to one side. 'Why all the cloak and dagger stuff?'

'Angel's convinced that Elke's whereabouts have to be kept secret,' he muttered back. 'This stalker incident in the bookstore has turned her paranoid.'

40

I could see why this had happened too, given that Angel Christian herself had been the victim of one of the most famous and vicious snatches in recent years. I guess now she saw kidnappers round every corner. 'That's why she was checking out the rooftops!'

Dad nodded quickly. 'And there may be more than she already told us.'

So we listened in again as Angel gave Elke her orders. 'You stay here. You don't take one step outside the building, got it?'

A scared Elke agreed.

'You realise why I moved you from my place? Heaven's Gate is too high profile; there'd be no chance of hiding you there for long. We needed somewhere more obscure, where no one would think to look.'

Behind Angel's back, Dad rolled his eyes at me. *Thanks, boss!*

'This is ideal,' she continued. 'A nice, homey little place, and you know, I would trust Sean and Katie with my own life!'

'*Kate*', not '*Katie*'! That really made me mad.

'Listen up!' Dad cut in, as if something had just struck him. 'What I don't understand is who exactly are we meant to protect Elke from? Is it the press getting on to her tail and hassling her while her mom's sick?'

Angel faced him with a condescending sigh. 'Did you ever hear the name Michael Weiss?' she asked cryptically.

Dad and I shook our heads.

'He's the guy the cops hauled down to Eighth Precinct yesterday evening, after the security guards brought them in. They slammed a couple of public disorder charges on him, but then guess what the crazy sergeant only goes and does? He releases this loonie on a five thousand dollar bail!'

I was struggling with the idea that Michael Weiss didn't sound like the name of Elke's father. Except, wait! No one knew Elke's second name. It was one of those closely kept secrets built up by the marketing people to enhance her image. So maybe her mother had reverted to her family name of Svennivig whenever the marriage had presumably ended, and the father's name actually was Weiss; who knows?

Angel was still on her high horse. 'I'd like to have seen that dumb sergeant's face when he heard the news that this same Michael Weiss had been spotted in Annika and Elke's hotel lobby just twenty minutes before this "accident"!'

I heard my dad take a deep, sharp breath and suddenly begin to take Angel more seriously. 'Did they pick him up and take him down the Precinct again?'

'Hell, no, and here's the problem.' Angel realised she had to spell out everything in plain English. 'It's what I've been trying to tell you. This stalker is a real psychopath, and he got away. I tell you, he's roaming the streets of Fortune City this very moment!'

All true, Elke told me in the privacy of our guest room. The guy had been trying to reach her. They'd heard he was in town about four days earlier. They knew the name he went under and that it was only a matter of time before he confronted them.

I was still trying to slow my thoughts down and stop my head from spinning.

Angel was gone; to another important meeting, she told us. Probably with her personal trainer or dietician. Dad was downstairs letting Fortune City General know in strictest confidence the number where Annika Svennivig's daughter could be contacted.

'Does this kind of thing happen often?' I asked Elke. 'I mean, stalkers, crazies . . . coming after supermodels?'

'All the time.' The eyes were dry and I realised that it wasn't kohl that darkened their rims in the photographs. It was a fringe of thick, black eyelashes. 'But this one's different.'

'So are you saying this Michael Weiss really did injure your mom?'

Elke sighed and shrugged. She cast about on the bed amongst the scattered contents of her purse for a paper tissue that was almost dry. Instead I fetched her one from the box in the shower room.

'Did anyone see the accident?' I pressed.

'No. Hotel Reception called up to our room to say a Michael Weiss was there to see us. Mom told me not to move and went down to deal with the problem.'

This made me stare hard. Annika Svennivig struck me as a gutsy woman, sure enough, but not stupid. Who in their right mind wouldn't have told Reception to call the police at this point? But no, Annika has to go and deal with the stalker personally.

'Ten minutes later I heard the ambulance siren, and I just knew right then that something terrible had happened. By the time I found out for sure, they'd put Mom in a body brace and stretchered her into the ambulance. A maid in the hotel had heard a loud crash on the service stairs and run to find her lying unconscious at the bottom of the stairwell.'

There wasn't a lot to say at the end of this. So I took Elke's hand in mine and thought real hard. I mean, I got it, but I didn't get it. There was still one giant question that I needed to ask.

And if you think this was all a bit out of my league, you'd be right. I had every intention of handing on this hot potato to the right people, the moment I'd got my all-important answer.

I took a deep breath and came out with it straight. 'So *is* Michael Weiss your father?'

Elke looked at me like I'd twisted a knife deep into her gut. She snatched her hand away, backed off against the wall, tried to frame a lie.

But she was too shocked that I knew.

'Yes,' she whispered in a cracked, little girl voice.

Carter and I had heard the guy right! 'Do the cops know?'

Shaking her head, she darted across the room and grabbed me by both arms. 'No! No, they don't! And they mustn't find out either from me or from you, you hear!'

I guess I've never seen such total panic in a person's eyes. It made me promise not to share the secret with a living soul.

'Except Joey Carter,' I warned her. That would be like calling water back up the faucet after it had splashed into the tub. 'I can't keep the information from him because he already knows the truth!'

4

You have to figure the chance of bumping into Elke's stalker two days after the launch party incident at three million to one. That's roughly the population of Fortune City.

But despite that, I'd have known it was the same guy, even without the facial cuts and contusions.

Me and Zig were watching the big ball game in Bruno's Diner on Twenty-first Street, close to where I live. It was Sunday, 4.30 p.m., when the human punch-bag walked in and naturally attracted a little unwelcome attention.

But this is Marytown, the old Italian quarter of the city, not southside or central. So you get quite a few guys coming into diners with broken noses and such like.

Bruno's was packed because of the wide-screen TV, and most people soon left off staring at the newcomer to concentrate on important stuff, like the Giants' latest signing.

Not me. I'd clicked in to what Zig calls my cop mode. He should know, since he has a brother in the Fortune

City force. I tell him that on a good day I might have the mental agility, but never the necessary hundred and fifty pounds of solid bone and muscle. I'm not proud of my physique, if you want to know.

Anyhow, I watched the stalker merge into the crowd at the counter. He ordered coffee like he needed something stronger but knew alcohol was not a good idea right now. Bruno studied the cut across the bridge of his nose as he slid the plastic coffee cup towards him. He must have made some mention of it, but the guy blanked him out and edged off into a dark corner.

The thought crossed my mind, as I took in the scuffed brown leather bomber jacket, the old jeans, the hollow cheeks and the unshaven chin, that if this really was Elke's father I could fully understand why she and her mom had been so quick to disown him. I mean, maybe he scrubbed up good, but right now he looked like home was a cardboard carton and a sleeping-bag under a dripping stone arch of Fortune's overhead train system.

You know that grey-white look, even in summer? And skinny, like food wasn't high on his list of priorities. His hands had the shakes, I noticed, as he raised the coffee cup to his lips.

Behind the counter, Bruno sizzled burgers on a griddle and stirred a big metal pot of fried onions. On the wide

47

screen, the new signing took time out, to loud protests from the crowd.

Meanwhile, the mystery man in the corner leaned over to pick up a used copy of the *Fortune City Times*. What he read on the front page didn't improve the nervous condition that was making his hands tremble like crazy. He leaned right forward over the newspaper, staring at the thing for much longer than it must have taken him to read the article.

Then he seemed to click out of the daze that had come over him and he jumped up from his chair. The metal legs scraped the floor tiles and the whole chair rocked into the guy at the table behind. But our stalker didn't stop to apologise; no way. He was in a hurry now. But not too much of a hurry to stop and tear off a corner of the front page of the newspaper and stuff it into his top pocket. Then he was on his way, stumbling against another table, pushing through the crowd at the counter, real close to where Ziggy and I stood.

So what had he read in our local *Times* on Sunday? As Zig cheered the return on court of the new signing, I reached past him to pick up another copy of the paper. Turning it back from the Sports pages to the headline on the front, I found myself going into the same startled huddle as the stalker had.

'Family Crisis for Elke!' I read in heavy upper-case letters. Then underneath, the fact that Annika Svennivig had been rushed to hospital the day before, where her condition was said to be 'comfortable', whatever that means. The journalist picked up on the mystery surrounding the incident: police were denying that they were treating it as suspicious; at the same time they were investigating the reported presence of a stalker at the scene only minutes before. As yet, there was no definite connection between the two circumstances.

Like, yeah! That looked pretty suspicious to me. Reading on, I found that supermodel Elke, who was in town for a book launch and a big fashion shoot, was said to be traumatised by the whole thing, but so far had had no direct contact with the media. A final paragraph told me that the not-normally-camera-phobic model had shunned photographers for the last twenty-four hours, but was said to be holed up in a house in the centre of town belonging to an employee of media mega-star, Angel Christian.

Zig must have wondered where I went. One second I was elbow to elbow with him in Bruno's, breathing in onions. The next I was on a Number 6 train to Constitution Square.

My first thought after I caught my breath and slumped into a seat was to pull out my new cell-phone (birthday present from my folks) and call the Brennans' number. No reply. So then I tried Heaven's Gate. It's in my 'Look-up' system because the Angelworks office is where I sometimes call Kate.

All I got on this occasion was a secretary guy.

'Angel has no comment on the current situation regarding Annika Svennivig and her daughter,' he parroted. Robot-man.

'Look, this is important!' I yelled down the phone. 'I need to know if my friend, Kate Brennan, is mixed up in this!'

'No comment,' he said, and briskly ended the conversation.

So, though there seemed to be no one home at Kate's house, I was committed to going there on the Circle train. I was still completely in the dark, but my gut told me that the answer I didn't get out of Angel's mechanical man was 'Yes'. This was just the type of thing that Kate would get herself mixed up in.

And if I could work this out from the information in the paper, then so could a crazy bum who claimed to be Elke's dad. Likewise any journo who halfway knew his job would too. So the Brennans' place in that quiet, refined square would most likely be crawling with press.

But no. When I jumped off the train and shot across the dual carriageway on State Hill to reach Constitution Square, things looked pretty normal. No crowds of cameramen, no police presence, no fugitive stalker; nothing.

I crossed the Square and ran up the stoop of number 18. Using mine and Kate's special code – two short presses, two long, two short – I leaned on the door buzzer.

If either Sean or Kate was lying low in there, they'd know it was me. It wasn't like we'd exactly planned this unique code; more like it had evolved as a friendly announcement of my arrival.

So anyway, I soon got Sean's voice on the intercom saying hi to me.

I spoke back. 'Sean, it's Joey! How come you're not answering calls?'

'Come in and I'll tell you.'

The heavy panelled door clicked open and I stepped into the house.

Sean greeted me in the hallway, dressed in crumpled T-shirt and jogging-pants. He looked tired and hassled. 'I just got rid of a pack of baying newsmen,' he told me. 'Not to mention this crazy Michael Weiss guy who came knocking at my door!'

Zoom – click! Things fell into place – better late than never. 'Does Michael Weiss wear a brown leather jacket and need a shave?' I inquired.

Sean shot me a sharp look. 'That's the guy. He tries to tell me he needs to see Elke. I attempt to close the door on him, but not before he's put his foot in the way. I still don't admit anything to him, even when he tells me that he's Elke's father.'

Wow, Kate and me had heard right! 'Is Kate here?' I asked. I didn't want any beating about the bush with Sean. 'Listen, I'm not asking you to say yes or no and break a promise, but my guess is that Angel chose this place to hide Elke from the press . . . ?'

Sean didn't contradict. He just kept on staring at me, letting me know he wasn't comfortable with any of this.

I went on, fast as I could. 'So this has put you under pressure. And I'm not exactly sure what's going down here, but I do say there's half a chance that this Michael Weiss guy is telling the truth about his family connection with Elke. Call it a gut feeling.'

'So what, Joey?' Kate's dad had let me have my say. 'Do you follow this press theory that Weiss was involved in Annika's accident?'

Here I shrugged. 'Who knows. But it makes it pretty

important that I talk with Kate. Like, I'm worried about her.'

'That my daughter has been dragged into the middle of something dangerous?'

Sean Brennan knew that this wouldn't be for the first time. And I knew he trusted my judgement quite a lot.

'OK, you win.' Frowning, he took me through to the kitchen and told me the story of how Elke had ended up at their house the night before. 'She was here until midday today, when the first journo got a whiff of our address. Then I called Angel and between us we decided that this wouldn't be a safe place for much longer.

'So Angel made a few more quick calls, got back in touch and informed us that her driver would be along incognito to collect Elke, take her to the fashion shoot that's been in her diary since May, and afterwards escort her to a new hiding place where the press wouldn't get hold of her.'

'Which is where?' I asked.

Sean shrugged. 'I'm not in on any of this. You'd have to ask the boss.'

'And can I talk to Kate?' was my next question. I was walking out of the kitchen towards the stairs, heading for her room.

'She's not here.'

I knew Sean wasn't lying and I felt my heart sink. 'So where is she?'

He knew I probably knew the answer. 'Elke got pretty close with Kate last night . . . Girl talk. By this morning it was clear they had things in common. You know, that poor kid looks like she has the world at her feet, but I was picking up a lot a bad vibes, besides the fact that her mom's in hospital.'

'Yeah, I agree.' I wanted to hurry Sean. 'So?'

'So she probably confided in Kate and trusted her to be her friend. That must have been the reason she asked Kate to go with her and help her unpack her stuff in the new place after she's finished the shoot.'

I caught up with Elke and Kate at the Virgin Building next to Fortune City Hall. They'd closed off the top floor for the whole of Sunday afternoon, ready for the glamour girl's arrival amid high security.

Of course, this explained the reason why the press weren't camped on the Brennans' doorstep. They were here instead. Which you'd think would create a problem getting Elke out of here again to a new safe house, until you realised that with her connections, Angel could airlift her out of the building in a private helicopter if necessary. Most newspapers don't have the hardware to match that.

Anyway, the usual security guards were stopping everyone from reaching the twenty-fifth floor. It was OK to mill around the music store downstairs, but not OK to use the elevators. I tried. Result: one bruised shin from the flying tackle employed by Gorilla Man Numero Uno.

'I need to speak to a friend,' I explained, hopping around the elevator lobby. I was in pain at the time. 'She's up there with Elke!'

'And my girlfriend is Linda Evangelista!' the guy who'd kicked me grunted back.

Dead end. Throbbing shin. But a cell-phone in my pocket, with Kate's mobile number programmed in. Why didn't I think of that earlier? Because it's a new toy, I guess (only three days since my birthday). And I'm not cool with the technology as yet.

Stabbing the buttons and fighting back the smarting sensation in my eyes, I waited to hear Kate's voice.

She'd read my number trying to call her, so there was no surprise when she finally answered. 'Joey, where are you?'

'Downstairs in the lobby.'

Now there was surprise. 'How come?'

I explained fast, with the gorilla still keeping me within crushable distance. 'Can you get me a pass to come up?' I asked Kate.

'Wait.' Cancel surprise. Inject determination. If I knew Kate, she'd be down with the necessary piece of paper within five minutes.

And sure, I was up with the celebs before the security guard could count to a hundred. Which in his case might have taken all of five minutes.

Not having been to a fashion shoot before, it took some time before I understood anything.

There were girls everywhere. If you'd pressed me, I wouldn't have been able to say which ones were models, make-up artists, hair stylists or photographers. Except the models walked about in underwear and steel hair clips. There were rails loaded with hangers, trolleys overflowing with hairbrushes, lip-gloss, cotton-buds, sponges, eyelashes, sprays . . . Don't ask me – it's a girl thing.

At last I made out Elke, who didn't look like she did last time I saw her. Today her long, straight hair was curled and short, her eyelids were shaded green and she was dressed from head to toe in a silver leather catsuit.

Kate dragged me across the set and made the introductions between shots, while the lighting men set up new angles. 'Elke, this is Carter. Remember, I told you about him?'

The supermodel greeted me suspiciously.

Well, I would too. Let's face it, I didn't look like I belonged amongst the Giannis, Horsts and Bruces.

'It's OK, Joey, I made Elke see that I couldn't keep you out of the Michael Weiss secret, even if I wanted to.' Kate tried to smooth things over by being her usual up-front self.

But this only deepened Elke's scarlet pout. As did my mumbled attempt at 'hi!'

Not a long word, I know. But let's go for the truth here; this kind of woman terrifies me, so I knew I wasn't going to be at my articulate best. I only hoped I wouldn't embarrass myself totally.

'Carter was worried about us,' Kate explained. I'd told her this much on the way up in the elevator. I'd also told her about seeing Weiss in the diner and his reaction to the front page. Also, that he must be pretty smart to have narrowed down so fast the unnamed 'employee' in the article to Sean Brennan. 'He thinks your father must be growing more desperate by the hour.'

If it was possible for Elke to turn any paler than she already was, she did right then. 'Are the cops gonna arrest him again?' she whispered. 'Do they think he attacked my mom?'

'You know more than we do,' I pointed out. 'I expect they talked to you after they found her unconscious.'

'Yeah, but that was yesterday. They said they couldn't

act on this Michael Weiss thing until Mom regained consciousness. They're waiting at her bedside right now.'

(Elke, by the way, seemed to be holding herself together pretty well on this score. I mean, not many kids could carry on with their high-pressure jobs with their mom in intensive care.)

'The cops don't realise that Weiss is related to Elke!' Kate warned me in a voice just above the inaudible.

I frowned and risked a full frontal glance at Elke, who returned the look with eyes of stone.

'It's complicated,' Kate put in.

A Marcel or a Frederick flitted by and waved a hairbrush in the direction of Elke's blonde curls. 'Davide wants you on set again,' he drawled.

So we watched Elke take up position and get her lip-gloss touched up under the lamps. Then they turned on a wind machine specially angled to riffle through some loose sheets of paper on a table. The sheets were meant to drift artistically into shot, and the machine made a humming noise which allowed Kate to carry on the explanations in private.

'Get this!' she whispered. 'Annika and Michael split when Elke was only a baby. So early she never had any memories of him; no photographs, no letters – zilch communication between her estranged parents. And she never knew the reason for this until about six months ago, when her father finally made contact.'

'With Annika or with Elke?' I watched the papers lift in the current of air and sift gently off the table, then cling to Elke's silver catsuit as she faced towards the machine. Her chin jutted out; she looked like she was all made of stone, not just her eyes.

'Definitely not with Annika,' Kate told me. She was getting worked up as she reached the real point of the story; her eyes were growing wider, she was leaning towards me, and that curtain of dark hair of hers was swinging against my bare arm. 'Weiss writes a letter to Elke, right? He says not to mention to her mother that he's been in contact. But that he has something important to tell her, which will help explain the reason for the break-up of the marriage. It's gonna affect Elke very deeply, so it's only something he can share face to face.'

By this time, I'm getting pretty tense myself. 'So?' I croak, as Davide's camera works overtime.

'So finally, after weeks of not knowing what to do, Elke does risk a secret meeting. This would be about the end of May. And to cut it short, she does discover this mind-blowing piece of information . . .'

Kate paused as a lighting guy came over and asked us to move from off his coils of cable. We found a new, more out-of-the-way corner between two rails of perfumed clothes.

'Spit it out!' I urged.

'The reason Weiss and Annika split is one you'd never guess . . .'

'Kate!' I practically grabbed her by the wrist.

'OK, OK! Listen! The two of them argued over a second kid called Gian, born just minutes after Elke. It turns out that Gian was about six months old when they diagnosed her with some serious medical problem which might mean she would never lead a normal life. Weiss wouldn't tell Elke exactly what it was, but he said at that point Annika was determined to turn her back on the problem. She wanted the baby sent off to a residential home or something. He didn't. So they separated. Annika kept Elke and Weiss went off with Gian. They never heard anything from him again until earlier this year.'

'And Elke never knew this?' I checked. This was enough to rock anybody's boat; suddenly discovering that you had a twin. A second version of you. How had she held it together, I wondered.

'Annika never breathed a word. But Elke knows Weiss was telling the truth.'

'How exactly?'

'He gave her a small packet containing two intertwined

60

curls of baby hair – pure gold – together with a scientific DNA report to show that one curl belonged to Elke and the other to a non-identical twin!'

'OK. So we're into June,' I said, pushing for a conclusion. 'And Elke confronts Annika with the truth, right?'

Kate nodded. 'Annika went crazy. She denied it all. She said she knew Weiss twenty years before, but that he was crazy then and he's crazy now. The DNA report was a fake. Then she put an absolute veto on Elke ever having any more contact with Weiss.'

I thought about this. 'Annika's a hard woman to argue with, I guess.'

'Right. So Elke's had to bottle this thing up ever since.' As she came to the end of the explanation, Kate stared across at the model who was still hard at work with her famous scowling mouth and moody lids, doing her best to form a relationship with Davide's camera lens. 'Is there any wonder she doesn't know how to smile?' she murmured.

Kate's a soft touch. She lets herself get involved in other people's problems. Like me. 'What happened to the twin?' I asked.

Kate's gaze didn't shift. She sounded sad as she delivered the answer. 'Still alive,' she sighed. 'Some place in the mid-west. Elke doesn't know where.'

5

'He's not gonna give in!' Elke stated what we all knew was true; that Michael Weiss's mission to stay in touch with her had become a genuine obsession.

We were in Robot-man's studio apartment in East Village, and it's a long story about how we came to be there; me, Carter and Elke.

Robot-man is Carter's name for Angel's secretary, Tom Hart. He was the latest victim of his employer's autocratic style.

'Tom, honey,' she'd wheedled over the phone. 'We have a little problem . . .'

To cut it short, Tom had agreed to turn his apartment into a new safe house for Elke, away from the glare of publicity. Not that he had any choice if he wanted to keep his job.

His place was on the fifth storey of a brownstone house on the fashionable side of town. It overlooked a cute, three-sided courtyard, and beyond that a green park where you could sit in open air cafés drinking cappuccinos. Inside the flat, Tom had knocked down walls and gone for open-plan. His decorator had chosen white for walls and soft furnishings, with big splashes of primary colour in throws and cushions. Pretty neat, but you had to take care where you stood your coffee cup.

In any other circumstances, you would've said it was a great place to be. But it wasn't the focus of our attention after a quick first impression.

Tom had gone into the kitchen to make us all an evening meal of pasta, before Carter headed for home. I'd arranged to stay over with Elke, though my dad didn't sound too happy about it on the phone. And that was when Elke came out with that comment about her father.

'He'd do anything to get in contact with me again,' she confessed to us as we sat in the wide window bay overlooking the park.

Staring down at the long shadows and people roller-blading across the diagonal paths, Joey and I nodded.

'I guess he thinks he has good reasons,' I said. 'Even the law would say he had a right to see his own daughter.'

'*If* the daughter wanted to see him,' Carter pointed out.

We both turned to stare at Elke.

There was a long pause, then a simple bottom line. 'I do, but I'm scared.'

'Of Weiss?' I pressed.

'Of what more he might tell me . . . about my sister. I mean, what was so dreadful about her that my mom wanted to send her away? Was the poor kid born with only half a brain, or something?'

This sounds harsh, but Elke didn't mean it that way. I could see she was imagining all sorts of deformities and tragedies for her disappeared twin. The thought made her tearful again.

'It sounds like you believe the DNA evidence?' It was Joey's turn to ask questions.

Elke nodded. 'Who would make it up? Why?'

'And your mom won't even let you talk about it, I guess?'

This time a shake of the head and a trembling hand over her eyes. 'You don't know Mom. Once she says a thing, you have to do it.'

'Well yeah, when you're a little kid,' Carter agreed. He really got stuck in to the topic. 'But not now. At this age, you have the right to choose.'

Which is when Elke looked up at him with her empty stare. Her eyes were blank; it was her mask-face.

'How come Annika has this influence?'

(Psychology-major Joey. I could just see him sitting behind his big, shiny therapist desk.)

Elke gave the superficial answer first. 'She's my mother, and she's also my agent. She fixes everything: planes, dates, destinations. Without her, I would most likely have been waitressing my way through college, training to be a junior school teacher.'

With Elke's face and body this was hard to imagine and I told her so.

Carter hardly let me finish my comment before he went on. 'So, she's your manager. But doesn't she care when she sees you unhappy over this Michael Weiss thing?'

There was a flicker of expression on Elke's face; a dark shadow behind her eyes. 'We don't talk about it.'

By which we understood that no, Annika didn't care. I was beginning to get a pretty nasty picture here.

'And so maybe Weiss was driven to trying something real stupid,' Carter suggested. He was edging towards the rumour that Annika's accident was no accident and that Weiss had attacked her on the hotel stairs. 'Like, for instance, if he could remove your mom from the picture, there would be no bar to his access to you.'

'I know what you're saying.' Elke sighed and looked

away. 'Y'know, I think if there was some kind of incident on the stairs, it might not have been as simple as that. Like, my mom has a real tendency to lose control. She could shout, she could hit out . . .'

I stood up and took a few steps across the room. In the kitchen, I could hear Tom Hart chopping and tossing things into a pan. I for one didn't feel much like eating.

Jeez, the picture was darkening by the second. Not as far as Weiss was concerned; he was a grown man and could take care of himself. But I was thinking abuse here; of one small, terrified child by one tall, super-dominant parent. Over a number of years.

'So Annika could've gotten into a fight?' I asked.

Elke shrugged. 'Maybe some kind of physical contact . . . who knows?'

For myself, personally, I couldn't stand any more of this talk. My imagination was running wild. As for Elke, she was stuttering and grinding to a halt. I figured that Carter was upset too.

Luckily – or maybe not – the phone rang at this point.

Tom carried it in from the kitchen and handed it to Elke. 'It's news from the hospital!' he hissed.

We stiffened and watched Elke's face.

The conversation was short. We heard her say, 'Yes . . . yes . . . yeah, OK, thanks.' Then she clicked off the phone. 'Mom regained consciousness,' she told us. 'They say she wants me to visit.'

This time Angel had done a good job of hiding Elke from prying eyes, so, with Tom driving us we made it to Fortune City General without attracting attention.

It was a ten minute trip, which I filled by asking Elke if there was a way – any way at all – that Joey and I might be able to help.

'For starters, how about we try to talk to Weiss ourselves?' I suggested. 'He may be off-limits to you, but there's nothing written down that says we can't meet him for you!'

It may not sound smart to have made the offer, because who knew what we were getting dragged into. On the other hand, you haven't experienced the full force of the despair on Elke's face.

'Or else!' Carter came in with his idea as we swung down State Hill towards the centre of town. 'Maybe we could put in a little work to trace Gian for you?'

Like, brilliant Carter! So simple; why didn't I think of that? We hear that the twin sister is alive and living in the mid-west. That only makes seven or eight states and a hundred million people plus to sift through!

Elke smiled gratefully at us, but we hadn't succeeded in rekindling any hope in those beautiful eyes. 'You two are sweet,' she told us absently, looking out through the car window at the high-rise block of hospital rooms, then picking out a handful of journalists camped out at the main entrance.

So Tom found a service entrance, where he dropped us off, promising to let the hospital staff know who we three kids were and why we were sneaking in up the linen and surgical supplies elevator. An intern in a white coat met us on Level 22 and led us along a squeaky cream corridor straight to Annika's room. I counted two cops at the door, two more inside the small intensive care unit.

One of these, a female sergeant, allowed Elke close to the bed, but stepped in front of Carter and me, silently warning us to keep our distance. She told Elke that her mom had been awake for forty-five minutes, but, apart from asking for her daughter, hadn't said a word to anybody.

Not that the patient wasn't fully aware of her surroundings. She lay strapped inside a neck and body brace, her face pale and gaunt above the collar, her eyes focused on Elke as she sat by the bed. 'Did you make it to the Virgin store for this afternoon's shoot?' she asked.

I know people have different responses in a crisis, but I thought this was fairly unique. I mean, you've almost lost your life, and the first thing you talk to your daughter about is work.

'Yeah.' Elke filled her in briefly, and told her that since Annika's accident, Angel Christian had been taking good care of her.

'Is that what they're saying?' Her mom's mouth stretched in a grim smile. ' "An accident", huh?'

The sergeant and the junior cop moved half a step closer. They let the reunion continue without interfering though.

Elke dodged the subject. 'Mom, what did the doctors say? Are you gonna be OK?'

'Too early for a prognosis. All I know is I'm strapped inside this damned cage for the duration!'

'Can you move your legs and arms?'

'Oh sure. I just jogged up and down the corridor, lifted a few weights and devised a new programme with my fitness instructor!'

'Not funny!' Elke looked round for a more informed medical opinion. The intern who had greeted us had just returned with a more senior doctor. By now the unit was jam-packed.

The older doctor took one look and began to empty the room. Carter and I were first out, followed by one of the cops. But before the door closed on us, we heard Annika countermand the order.

'No, let everyone stay!' she called out. 'I need plenty of witnesses for the statement I'm about to make.'

That made us stop short and turn right around.

'About this "accident" ,' Annika went on, taking hold of Elke's hand in a gesture that didn't seem to contain much affection. The grip was too hard and it proved there was no impairment to the function of her upper body. Likewise her strong, clear voice and her memory. 'I'm not here due to any accident. This was deliberate.'

I saw Elke slump forward and at the same time try to squeeze her hand out of Annika's grasp.

'Are you describing an attack, Mrs Svennivig?' the sergeant asked. 'If so, could you come across with an account of the incident?'

Annika obliged in a monotone. 'I left the hotel room and took the elevator to Reception. I stepped out of the elevator and straight into Michael Weiss, who stuck a gun in my ribs and ordered me out of the main door, around the back of the hotel to the parking lot. There wasn't a lot I could do, until a guy in a delivery truck started up his engine and then I risked a run for it, knowing Weiss wouldn't shoot in front of a witness. I made it inside the service entry, up two flights of stairs before he caught up with me, pinned me against the rail with the gun to my head this time.'

'What did you do, Mrs Svennivig? Did you scream? Did you resist?' The sergeant absorbed every detail, glancing at her junior to make sure he was writing it all down.

Annika stared back from the bed, only her eyes moving from face to face in the room. 'If I'd resisted a gun to my temple I'd be dead by now,' she said slowly. 'It was only at the last split second that I realised his plan wasn't to shoot me but to push me over the rail into the stairwell and make it look like an accident.'

The cop nodded. 'So what's the last thing you remember?'

'His face, real close to mine. His whole body weight pushing me back then . . . nothing.'

It sounded real, the way she said it.

And it made the cops decide to pick up Michael Weiss just as fast as they could.

'Don't let the girl out of your sight,' the sergeant told the two on duty outside the door as Elke said her goodbyes, ready to leave her mom to get some rest. 'The guy sounds like some kind of psychopath.

There's no predicting what he'll do.'

Shivers were running through my body as I helped Elke down the corridor and Joey followed close behind. We'd reached the elevator, expecting Tom Hart to pick us up downstairs and for the cop car to follow us back to his place. Now though, it didn't seem important to evade the press, since DI Greenwood, the sergeant's superior down at Eighth Precinct, was currently updating the media on the latest developments and appealing for witnesses. Pretty soon every journalist in the state would be crawling all over us.

Elke had turned stone cold after the session with her mom, and was shivering in spite of the sun when we came out of the building and looked around for Tom.

Maybe she had a premonition of what was coming, but it took the rest of us totally by surprise.

First, there was Tom's car cruising round the parking lot towards us. Then a figure sprang out of a nearby pick-up and began sprinting towards us. I recognised Weiss at the moment the cops drew their guns.

'Don't shoot!' Elke screamed. She broke free from the group and ran towards Weiss.

The cops' aim dodged and dived, but they couldn't fire their weapons in case they hit Elke.

It was only when Tom drove his car between Weiss and Elke that things slowed down. It gave Carter and me time to chase Elke and the cops time to fan out and try to corner Weiss against a tall wire fence.

Above the screech of tyres and the sound of running feet, Weiss was yelling at Elke over the hood of the skidding car. 'Durango!' He named the same town two, three times so there could be no mistake. 'Durango! Durango! Go there!'

'Don't shoot him!' Elke was begging the cops. She was practically scrambling over the car to reach him as the cops came up behind. 'He doesn't have a gun. Please don't shoot!'

Their own guns glinted, their dark uniforms closed in.

Weiss knew his situation was hopeless. 'Find Joelene and Ed Foster!' he yelled at Carter and me. 'You got that?'

It was all he had time for before the cops finally jumped him. No bullets, just a professional job of rushing him against the fence and pinning both arms up his back. The arrest was over before you knew it.

6

Well, Weiss had narrowed it down for us. Now all we had to do was find a couple called Ed and Joelene Foster in a town called Durango in the south west of Colorado.

Fine, no problem.

Meanwhile, Weiss was in custody. Annika Svennivig was having X-rays and scans in Fortune City General. Kate was staying with Elke at Robot Tom's place. Oh, and it was Monday, and I was rollerblading in City Park with Fern and my kid brother, Damien.

'Joey, these kids are climbing the walls down here – will you please get them out of my hair and take them to the park!' Mom had yelled up the stairs while I was brushing my teeth. I'm slow to get out of bed during the summer vacation. I mean, I work three nights a week at the local Eight Til Late (Mom got me the part-time position), so I reckon I deserve these late mornings.

Mom didn't see it my way. That's how come Damien, Fern and me were rollerblading down Monument Hill.

And I was hot. The sun was beating down and anyone

with half a brain was sitting in the shade drinking ice-cold coke. Like Zig, Zoey and Connie. No way did they volunteer to don a pair of blades and help me entertain the kids.

'Move it, Joey!' Damien was eight years old and way ahead of me in the rollerblading department. Fern likewise. My dad always said the kid must've been born with a set of wheels attached to her feet. So they were weaving in and out, overtaking me on the hill, leaning into the bends and executing all these cute flips and turns. Meanwhile I was trying to look cool and laid back, just coasting along.

At least it gave me thinking time. Space inside my head, sitting on the edge of what looked like a pretty explosive situation in the world of supermodels.

Check it out with me. This Weiss trying to kill Annika thing: the allegation is that he met her in the hotel lobby and jammed a gun in her ribs, terrorised Ice-Queen mom out into the parking lot, where only the fortunate intervention of a guy in a truck starting up his engine prevented Annika's brains from ending up in a space reserved for hotel guests.

To me this didn't quite figure.

In this scenario, Weiss comes across as a gun-crazed maniac. So where was his gun yesterday, when he jumped out of that old pick-up at the hospital and made his last ditch bid to reach Elke? No sign of gun-craziness there, and that was exactly the kind of situation where any self-respecting maniac could use a shooter.

No, the chances are, guns aren't Weiss's style.

Also, no delivery-truck driver from the hotel had come forward to report an incident of a crazy guy chasing a woman through the service door. Yet the case had attracted a whole heap of media attention, and unless the truck driver was illiterate, or maybe just passing through the planet, he would've read about it in the press.

So what if the incident didn't happen the way Annika told the cops? I mean, I know it sounds bad to suspect a woman laid up in hospital inside a total body-brace of lying, until you recall that her own daughter was the first to bring up the possibility.

Switch the scene around. Imagine. We know Weiss is desperate to see Elke and tell her the whole story of her twin sister in Colorado. We also know that Annika keeps a stranglehold on her daughter's activities and is denying that she ever gave birth to twins. So someone's lying there. Say it's Annika again.

So the scene in the lobby goes like this: Momma goes down to deal with Weiss. She doesn't want any of the hotel staff poking into her family stuff, so she persuades Weiss to come with her to a more private place, like the service area round the back. They argue, and she's the one who loses it. She gets physical with Weiss. He has to defend himself. It all gets so crazy on the stone stairway that in the end Annika loses her footing, slips and falls.

Now she's lying in the stairwell unconscious. This is enough to force anyone to make a rapid exit, especially someone like Weiss. I mean, the cops are already charging him with minor offences regarding Annika and Elke.

'Joey, get out of the way!' Damien yelled. He swerved round me with Fern on his heels. They're pushing 30 mph on the final downhill stretch.

I lost my cool, wobbled and ground to a halt.

Yeah! I thought. *The bottom line is not to believe a word Annika Svennivig says. Monster Momma. Harsh but true.*

And then there was a pleasant interruption in the shape of Kate walking along the path towards our tree.

Fern saw her arrive before me and threw herself at her. Those two get along great. Fern gets all the hugs and kisses. I just stand and watch.

So the big news was the latest on the Elke situation, and by the time I joined the group Kate had already informed Zig, Zoey and Connie that Annika would have to spend at least three weeks in hospital.

'That's the bad news,' she told them as she sat cross-legged on the grass. She acknowledged me with a worried smile. 'The good news is, the doctors are saying no major damage to the spinal column. Severe concussion, a couple of vertebrae crushing against a disc in the lower back, but nothing that complete bed rest and a programme of physiotherapy won't put right.'

'Lucky!' Connie whistled. She knew about backs and discs. I reckon she'll go to college and study chiropractice; body posture, bones, alternative health issues. It's her kind of thing. 'The woman falls two storeys and gets off with a compressed disc!'

'If we believe what she told the cops,' I put in, ready to share my latest theory.

Con, Zoey and Zig ignored me. They wanted more info from Kate.

'How's Elke doing?' Zoey asked in a concerned voice, like she and the supermodel were best buddies.

'She's doing OK,' was Kate's guarded reply.

When someone swears Kate to secrecy, you can bet your bottom dollar she'll keep her word. None of that loose, confidential talk like a lot of girls get into.

'Work pressure is lousy, though. She's due to fly out to Tokyo tomorrow, and Annika is making it clear that she still needs to go. It's some big deal to promote a major perfume for the biggest designer in Japan, worth . . .' She hesitated over giving away even this much of Elke's private business.

'. . . Big bucks?' I suggested.

'Yeah,' Kate sighed, then smiled.

'Private joke?' Zoey enquired. That girl has built-in radar for romantic nuances, believe me.

'Not a joke exactly,' Kate said. 'Anyhow, the really big news is, the cops have charged Weiss with attempted homicide.'

Connie greeted this big news as no news. 'Sure,' she shrugged. 'They'd be crazy not to, with that kind of evidence staring them in the face.'

'You mean his history of stalking Elke?' Zoey joined in with enthusiasm. 'That kind of guy is real sick, don't you think? I mean, what normal guy would get so obsessed with a celebrity that he follows them all over the country, like they say Weiss has? I read in the paper that some shrink thinks he probably suffers full-blown delusions; stuff like being genuinely in love with the object of his obsession, or in this case, being Elke's father!' She laughed like this was truly weird.

Kate and I got real busy with a loose strap on one of Fern's boots. Kate held the kid in her lap while – *sschhkk*

– I pulled the velcro loose, tightened the strap and – *psshhmm* – refastened it.

I heard Zig groan 'Oh, man!', his sole contribution to the discussion of Michael Weiss's weirdness. Otherwise he just lay on his back, staring up at the pattern of leaves against a pure blue sky.

Connie and Zoey were deep into the celebrity stalker topic. They drew high-profile comparisons, recalled tragic outcomes, starting with John Lennon way back.

'Carter, let's walk,' Kate said abruptly, after about five minutes of this. 'I told Elke I'd hurry back.'

Zoey picked up on this straight off. The fact that she didn't say anything, but raised her eyebrows and exchanged significant looks with Connie, spoke louder than words.

'I have to take care of Fern and Damien,' I told Kate. Who'd have kid brothers and sisters at a time like this?

'That's OK, Joey, you go ahead with Kate,' Zoey jumped in. 'Zig and me will make sure the kids are OK.' More meaningful looks. I swear that girl's eyebrows are gonna meet up permanently with her hairline one day soon.

So anyway, I accepted, gave Damien a couple of dollars for cold drinks and made my exit with Kate.

'You need to talk?' I guessed, as we hit Constitution Hill and headed for the Circle Train.

'Carter, things are looking bad for Weiss.' She took the metal steps two at a time as a train drew into the station. 'He's in a his-word-against-hers situation, and if you look at him and Annika side by side, who are you gonna believe?'

'Yeah.' The carriage doors slid open and we both stepped inside. Hanging on to the overhead straps, swaying against each other as the train took bends at speed, I gave Kate my theory about Weiss not being the gun-crazed psychopath that Elke's mom had painted.

'No, but image is the problem here.' Kate had obviously thought about this as thoroughly as me. 'He looks like a bum. And from what he confessed to Elke, his history's not too impressive either.'

'Does he have criminal convictions?'

'A couple. Small-time stuff; stealing from a drug-store, occasionally getting thrown out of a bar and being picked up drunk. That's his problem: alcohol. No violence though.'

The few details I was being fed built up a lousy picture: not much of a life. Dead-end jobs, drinking binges, unemployment, drifting. I could be describing a million seedy lives in a thousand American cities.

The train jolted to a halt at the station we needed for Robot Tom's place, so we got off. I was prepared to walk the tree-lined sidewalks with Kate, then split off when we reached the apartment.

'Elke's going crazy,' Kate told me. 'She stayed awake all last night explaining things. The stupid thing is, she's the innocent party here, yet she's the one who feels guilty.'

'How come?'

'I suppose for not standing up to her mom over this Michael Weiss stuff.'

I was quiet, trying to work this out. Like, you have Monster Momma and a drunk for a father; and the kid's the one who ends up feeling like it's *her* fault!

Kate paused at the entry to Tom's apartment block. 'Carter, don't you think we should do something to help?'

Like head for the nearest phone booth and change into my Superman costume? Like, run a cloaked crusade against the whole Fortune City police force, not to mention the mighty American justice system?

'Don't give me your cynical shrug!' Kate protested. She took offence. 'OK, Joey, forget it. Pretend I never opened my mouth. See you!'

I was up the steps ahead of her, backing through glass doors into the lobby. 'What did I say?'

'Nothing. You don't have to.'

'I'm here, OK? I'm listening!'

Kate's real sussed. She knows how to keep me in the

team. Anyhow, I was beside her there in the elevator, zooming up to Robot Tom's Ideal Home.

'Did you ever feel helpless?' Elke asked us. 'I mean, truly, one hundred per cent trapped?'

There were clothes scattered over the floor, half in and half out of suitcases. And sprays, brushes, cosmetics lying on her bed. She was packing for her Tokyo trip.

'Yeah,' I said, standing hands in pockets by the door.

'A hundred times,' Kate added.

'And before you say anything; no, I don't have any choice about going to Japan.' Elke looked at me like I was bound to contradict her.

I acknowledged that plans had been made, contracts signed, plane tickets bought. Not to go would be to let too many people down.

'So try not to worry,' Kate said. 'Think positive. Your mom turns out not to be badly hurt after all. And maybe the cops won't be able to make the charges against your dad stick.'

She's good at building bridges over troubled waters, but not good enough this time.

Elke sighed and zipped up a cosmetics purse, tossed the whole thing in the case. 'They'll convict him. He'll get ten years in jail. And I don't get to meet my sister, and I carry on facing the camera, walking the catwalks, and what the heck . . .'

'Unless your mom has a change of heart.' Give Kate ten out of ten for trying. 'Maybe she'll come clean about what really happened after you were born.'

'If she had a heart to change,' Elke said softly.

End of story.

The girls said goodbye and a minder arrived at the apartment to help get Elke ready to leave for Japan.

There were a few tears. Like I said, Kate has a soft heart.

Mine was sinking too as we pressed the elevator button and went down to the ground floor. There's a lot of talk of hearts right here, because that's what was getting beaten up by the situation. Elke's, Kate's. My own angle was that I couldn't bear to see Kate look so down.

'We have to do something!' she said as we stepped out into the courtyard. There was a trellis covered with vines against one wall, a canvas canopy over the sunny side of the yard, with people and dogs sitting taking a rest. 'Do something!'

'Not your problem,' I tried to tell her. It was like talking to the vine-covered wall.

She withered me with her scorn. That's what they say in books. It feels lousy, believe me.

'I got it,' she went on, as if talking to herself, but knowing I was tagging along behind. 'What we do is find the twin sister!'

Brilliant, Einstein! I'd already zapped that idea off the map. But I ran tripping up over Kate's heels like a lapdog.

'It's what Weiss said we should do. It figures. If we reach Gian, we get the other half of the story. It fills in a lot of empty spaces for Elke, and it might even help get Weiss off the hook if that bit of the story proves correct!'

Yeah, I got all this. But . . . 'What do we have to go with?' I asked, running around to face Kate, then walking backwards down the sidewalk. 'Two names. A town. Nothing else!'

Which was how come, thanks to a generous monthly allowance from Kate's mom, it was Tuesday and Kate and I were sitting side by side on an American Airlines 747.

I was in the window seat, looking down on the Rocky Mountains and the pilot was instructing passengers to fasten their seat belts because we were coming in to land in Denver, Colorado.

7

Denver. They call it the Mile High City.

They designed the airport like a string of giant bedouin tents, each rising to a tall peak to echo the mountains behind.

This sounds like travel ad speak, but it happens to be true. It's fabulous and unique. Except that the airport authority has problems with the day-to-day running of the trains that link the terminals, and the only place to run if there happens to be a tornado in that part of the world is the ladies' rest rooms. No joke.

Joey thought Denver airport was cool. He strode ahead of me, bag slung over his shoulder, taking that loose, bouncing stride he has across the marble concourse. He was staring up at the overhead peaks and asking me, did I know what kind of material they were fabricated from: extruded plastic . . . polycarbonate . . . was it flexible or rigid?

That's the great thing about Carter: you can be slam in the middle of a crisis, and he talks about engineering.

86

Meanwhile, as Joey stared at the roof and bumped into the Hertz car hire desk, I was considering how to find Ed and Joelene Foster, talk with Gian, get the new info to Elke and leave her to decide what to do next. Between the two of us, I'm the one with my feet on the ground, but then you know that already.

The place to start was the Greyhound bus depot. It was a little after midday and we faced another eight hours in the scorching heat. Denver is north-east Colorado, Durango is south-west, so Carter and I climbed on the bus, then hid for the first half of the journey behind our reading matter: a glossy magazine in my case, a book on sporting heroes in Joey's.

When we'd read these from cover to cover, we exchanged them, and soon we were on the Interstate 550, passing through Telluride before I could say Michael Jordan.

This was Mesa Verde National park country, and if you don't know it, you need to think Clint Eastwood movies. Tall, crumbling fingers of red rock casting long shadows over the scrub. A dry wind raises the dust and blows the tumbleweed across the screen. Our hero faces the desert, alone except for his horse and a long, dark cigarette hanging from the corner of his mouth. A banjo twangs out a mournful tune. In Clint's narrowed eyes and tense jaw you see that he knows that out there somewhere are half a dozen Mexicans whose one murderous intent is to gun him down.

It's part of the great myth of the American West; empty land, scorching heat. Men in big hats and ponchos.

Unfortunately, from the Greyhound bus, I saw that not much of the legend remained among the Pizza Huts lining the interstate. Maybe a big neon sign in the shape of a sombrero advertising a cheap motel, a town called Chimney Rock, another sign showing the tourists how to reach the Anasazi Heritage Centre.

After Telluride, the road keeps on heading south for Durango (population 12,400), situated on the Animas River, a year-round destination for travellers, featuring a vibrant student community attending Fort Lewis College and the major attraction of the Durango and Silverton Narrow Gauge Railroad. I quote from the slightly outdated tourist guide Carter borrowed from the passenger in front.

No travelling the narrow gauge for us, I told him. No mountain biking, white-water rafting, kayaking or horseback riding while we were in town. We had our work cut out.

* * *

That evening we ate pizza on Main Street, paid thirty dollars each for two rooms at the Trail's End Motel, checked the phone lists and found twenty-three families named Foster in a population of just over twelve thousand. Only four of these had first names beginning with 'E', so we went to bed feeling pretty confident that before Wednesday was through, we'd have pinpointed Ed and Joelene, no problem.

'This place is like a film set.' Carter's first impression of Durango in the daylight wasn't exactly enthusiastic. He's an urban kid, comfortable with the feel of paving slabs under his feet and the sight of high-rise blocks to either side.

Durango looks like it still has one foot in the nineteenth century. Main Street has boardwalks and clapboard houses, and the gift shop windows are stacked with models of steam locomotives and cuddly mountain bears.

'It's an OK place to grow up in, I guess.' I was thinking of Gian, imagining her going to school on the modern campus on the far side of the river, maybe staying in a house with a driveway, space for three family cars and a swimming-pool round the side like the one we were approaching now.

'E.J. Foster, 1228 Navajo Drive' was the first E.

Foster on our list of four. My idea was that we needed to call on each one in person, to get a feel for whether or not we were on the right track. So, with a twenty-five per cent chance that we could hit lucky first time, I walked up the drive and knocked the door with a thumping heart.

'Ed Foster?' Carter asked the ancient guy in golfing shoes and a canary yellow sweater who came out on to the porch.

I was thinking, *No way! He's all of eighty years old, which would have made him early sixties when Gian had been put up for adoption.* Supposing that was the situation we had here. I mean, why else would Weiss have told us to trace the Fosters in order to find Gian? Both Carter and I automatically assumed that adoption was what Elke's down-and-out father had resorted to when he discovered he was incapable of taking care of the kid himself.

'Who wants to know?' The old guy wore a frown so deep it practically made his eyes disappear behind his heavy white eyebrows.

I gave him our names, noticed an old grey dog come limping out of the house and begin to sniff in a hostile fashion at the soles of Carter's shoes.

I think Joey took offence at the mutt. It was the

smelly, barrel-shaped kind with wiry hair and eyebrows like its owner's. 'Listen, mister,' he snapped back at the old guy. 'We only want to know if your name is Ed.'

Yeah, Carter. No medals for diplomacy there.

'Scoot right now, or I'll call the cops!' Mr Foster yelled.

The mutt growled and grabbed hold of the leg of Joey's pants. It held on tight as he lifted his foot and tried to shake it off.

Which naturally made the old guy even madder. 'Good boy, Buster! Hold fast! Maisy, you hear me? Pick up that phone, get Sergeant Nighthorse out here fast!' he yelled at his invisible wife inside the house.

A window blind twitched shut and the lady must have hurried off.

'Maisy!' As Carter shook himself free from the dog's incisors, I repeated the name. Not *Joelene*. 'Wrong place!' I hissed, ready to beat a retreat on to Navajo Drive.

We made a run for it then; out on to the tree-lined avenue, hotly pursued by one barrel-shaped dog. It had short legs and was dietetically challenged, so we soon outpaced it. By the time we hit East Fifth Street we were alone.

'One down, three to go!' I grinned at Carter. I couldn't help it when I remembered the look of terror on his face and realised I'd just learned a new fact about him: that he didn't have a natural affinity with the canine species.

'I never knew you were scared of dogs,' I mentioned casually as we got out our street plan and looked for Camino del Rio.

'Only when they have their teeth sunk into my ankle bone,' he pointed out. 'Listen, we have to take a left turn for the river, walk two blocks down Ninth Street and take a right on to Camino del Rio.'

'Stabbing the map with your finger does nothing to restore your macho image in my eyes,' I teased, snatching the sheet away then walking ahead. 'Maybe you should let me do the talking this time.'

'Feel free,' he mumbled, slouching along after me, reminding me that he'd never really wanted to come in the first place.

I pulled the list of four names from my pocket, crossed off 'E.J.' and scanned down. 'The E. Foster we plan to visit next is a doctor,' I told Joey. 'Maybe you could ask him to take a look at the leg, check you out for rabies and all that stuff.'

He ignored me. 'Doctor, huh? That's the kind of

guy who might take in a kid with a disability like Gian. It'd figure, wouldn't it?'

Hopes rising, we turned down Camino del Rio, which ran parallel to the Animas River. Here the houses were even larger and more countrified than on Navajo Avenue. They were spaced out and their gardens ran down to the water's edge, where there was room for boat sheds and small launches. At the back of all that, across the crystal clear river, rose a range of hills called the Tamarees which folded into Montezuma Valley and the Mesa Verde beyond.

'Nice place,' I murmured, hoping that this was the life that poor, rejected Gian had led. If a kid could fall on her feet like this . . . like Fern with the Carters . . . then maybe being adopted wouldn't be so bad.

But Dr E.L. Foster was Dr Elaine Linda Foster, a grey-haired geologist living alone in her log house, without even a dog to annoy us. She listened, she tried to make helpful suggestions, but no she was sorry, she didn't know an Ed and Joelene Foster.

'I only bought this house last fall,' she told us. 'I gave up my job in the Alaskan oilfields and looked for a place as different from Alaska as I could possibly find. Some place hot, with trees, and rivers that don't freeze over.'

We thanked her anyway and hoped she had a nice life on the Camino del Rio. Carter told her if it was sun she was looking for, Durango was the right choice.

'It's hot!' he complained, as we headed back in to town. His T-shirt stuck to his shoulders, there were beads of sweat along his hairline.

So we dived into a store selling ice-cream and gorged on a couple of mint chocolate chip specials, knowing that we had a walk right across town to reach E. Foster number three, with the initials E.P. and an address I'd written down from the phone book as 77 Twenty-fifth Street.

It was to the north, with a view of the narrow gauge railway running along the edge of its back garden. The houses were smaller, but still quaint and neat, with sprinklers switched on along all the front lawns.

'This feels like it.' Carter looked up at number 77; nothing remarkable in the gabled clapboard house with a carved awning over the porch and closed wooden shutters across the windows. He pointed out a cane swing in the porch, whose cushions were scattered with CD cases featuring the type of music a seventeen-year-old girl might listen to.

But before we could get it together to knock on the

door, a woman came down the side of the house next door.

'You looking for Amber?' she said.

'Yeah,' Carter said, quick as a flash.

(OK, so Gian could have had a name change here. She could be Amber Foster now. Only it took my slow brain longer to work this out.)

'You friends of hers?' the woman asked. Mrs Nuisance Neighbour, poking her face in. She was tall, dressed in loud lycra shorts and she carried too much weight.

'Yeah.' Joey said later that it depended on your definition of 'friend'. We wanted to help Gian, for sure.

'She went out.' Arms folding across her chest, a suspicious look dawning, Mrs Know-all slowly registered the fact that she'd never seen us in her life before.

'Who with?' Joey again. Cool now, and not about to lose it again.

'Joelene took her along to the hot springs.'

Yes! I felt my whole body jerk into super-alert status. *Joelene Foster. Amber. And presumably, some place around here . . . Ed!*

'Which ones?' Carter tried to keep it casual, but his pulse rate had obviously shot up too.

'The place Joelene works, of course.' The woman suggested we were stupid to ask, but being such a know-all she couldn't resist giving us the answer.

'Is that the Iron Horse Hot Springs or the Tamaree Springs?' Joey acted like he couldn't remember.

I admired him for remembering those two names off the town map.

'Tamaree. Look, here comes Ed now. Ask him where his daughter is, why don't you?' The Neighbour from Hell spotted a car pulling up at the kerb and made out like she had no more time to chat. She whipped a set of keys out of her shirt pocket, opened the door of the car parked on her own drive. Then, orange shorts and fat pink legs still protruding, she dived inside as if she was raking through clutter on the back seat for something important.

Some feeling told me to back off from asking any more questions. I jerked my head at Joey and we made it to the end of the driveway before Ed P. Foster got out of his car.

He spotted us and advanced. 'Yeah?'

Behind the monosyllable I got the strong impression that what he was really saying was, 'What the hell are you two no-good kids doing on my goddam property?'

Ed Foster was about as wide as he was tall. His belly

hung over his belt, and his walk was a fat man's walk, feet splayed, thighs rubbing together. He wore rimless glasses, and his thatch of almost black, wavy hair was slicked straight back from his sweating face.

This description doesn't give a nice effect, I know. But then, neither did the guy himself.

'Whad'ya-want?' he drawled. Behind the glasses, the eyes had pink rims which blinked frequently. He looked very myopic.

'Nothing. Sorry. Wrong house number.' I dragged Carter off by the elbow before he got into investigation mode.

Then I scooted him off along the street, suspecting it wouldn't be too long before Mrs Lycra-shorts let Ed know that we had in fact been two smartass kids asking personal questions about Joelene and Amber.

Joey didn't argue. Top of his list now was to hotfoot it to Tamaree Springs. 'You wearing your bathing costume?' he wanted to know.

'Yeah, why?' I often wore a two-piece beneath my T-shirt and shorts when the weather was this hot and there were cool pools to swim in. But that was personal.

'You'll need it to merge in with the crowd at the Springs.' He told me the new plan: pay the entry fee, mingle, take a good look around. It was all worked out by the time we approached the busy turnstile.

'Wow, now I really feel as if I'm on vacation!' I was in line for the hot springs with crying babies and moody looking six year olds.

Through the gates, we walked into a changing area, split off, took off most of our clothes and met up again by the side of the first open air pool. We picked our way through the muddle of arguing families and entwined lovers who cluttered up the edge of the pool, and I for one was wondering how we'd pick out Joelene and Amber, even if they were still here.

Oh, and I wasn't concentrating too well. Carter without most of his clothes is a big distraction.

'Joelene Foster has a job here,' he reminded himself, checking out the woman taking money at the turnstile and a guy rearranging sprinkler jets on a stretch of lawn beyond the pool complex.

'Maybe in the coffee shop,' I suggested.

So we worked slowly along the side of the next pool, then cut across towards the hot spring area and the cafe beyond. There were fewer people in the hot springs, all looking like boiled lobsters, but evidently lapping up the health-giving effects of the warm mineral water which bubbled up from far underneath the Tamaree Hills. It gurgled and bubbled around their wallowing torsos, popping and swilling, fizzing and giving off small gasps of warm, odourless air.

'People soup,' Carter muttered under his breath. Obviously not his thing.

But by this time I wasn't really listening.

I'd picked out a figure in the crowd. There was a girl lounging on a pool chair, the headrest set back, her long, slim body covered in cream and soaking up the sun. She was blonde, long-limbed and beautiful behind the dark shades.

'Incredible!' I whispered.

Carter followed the direction of my gaze.

No one else was staring at the girl in the black two-piece the way we were.

I mean, we couldn't take our eyes off her.

There was the straight, small nose in profile, the wide slash of full, Julia-Roberts lips. Plus the Scandinavian coolness, the aloofness that cried out movie-star, supermodel . . . *Look at me!*

I glanced at Carter, whose jaw had dropped. Then I got back to staring. Unbelievable! Impossible to get my head around . . . if I hadn't known for sure that there was half a continent and an ocean between us, I would have said without a shadow of a doubt that the girl on the sun lounger was Elke.

8

No, I wouldn't call Gian identical with Elke.

I argued with Kate about this as we sat up to our necks in warm water.

'She's not plastic,' I said.

'Plastic? What do you mean, plastic?'

The girl on the sun lounger had natural blonde hair, she didn't wear make-up or gel, or any of that gunk. To give it to you straight, she didn't wear much at all.

'C'mon, Carter,' Kate insisted as I continued to stare from my new position in the hot spring pool. After recovering from the initial shock of seeing Amber, we'd both flung our hired towels and valuables down on the grass and plopped gently into the spa pool. 'Give me one real difference between the girl on that lounger and the supermodel in all the magazines!'

'Shorter hair,' I pointed out.

'That doesn't count. I mean, one genetic variation.'

I was struggling to find one, but I was lucky. The girl in question removed her sunglasses and looked our way. I was able to see that her eyes were a light grey. 'Eye colour,' I told Kate.

Elke's are shining and rich, like dark honey. I know this from close study of the Face.

'Hmm.' No argument there. Then Kate switched tactics. 'But in any case, we know from Elke and the DNA test that they're not identical!'

'So why talk about it?' I knew we were wasting time here. Also that Kate grew spiky whenever I ogled the glamour twins. I took this as a good sign for the future.

Kate sighed and lifted one leg clear of the surface. Warm water trickled between her toes and dropped from her heel back into the pool. 'OK, so we know we've found the right person,' she conceded. 'This is definitely Elke's twin sister, so that part of Weiss's story turns out to be one hundred per cent true.'

'Except for one thing.' And this confused me. 'Y'know Michael Weiss said Annika rejected Gian because they discovered she had some type of disability?'

Kate was already thinking the same thing. 'I remember. And what you're saying is, there doesn't look to be a thing the matter with this girl.'

Perfect in every way, I would have said. But I refrained. 'Maybe the doctors cured her?'

'But it would have to have been something real awful

for Annika to react the way she did; a permanent mental condition maybe.'

I agreed. 'So they'd diagnose this illness pretty early and tell the family there was no cure. But it wouldn't necessarily be clear to the outsider. I mean, she could still look . . . normal.'

We're treading dangerous ground here. I don't know much about mental disability, or the terms they use to talk about it. It's easy to say the wrong thing and sound cruel.

'So where's Joelene?' Kate too gave up on this line. All we both knew so far was that Gian/Amber turned out to be as beautiful as her famous sister.

'Still busy, I guess.' I was thinking hard, reckoning that it was unusual for a girl Amber's age not to be hanging out with other kids. There were plenty around the poolsides, but none were paying her any attention.

'What do you say we go and talk to her?' The fact that Kate paused to ask me the question indicated that she wasn't sure.

'No, that might blow it.' I hesitated too, don't ask me why.

Anyhow, I immediately experienced a mega-embarrassing interruption.

My cell-phone played me a tune.

'The Stars and Stripes Spangled Banner' beeped at me from the grass, from beneath my scrunched up towel. Jeez; trust Damien for programming in that call tone!

It meant I had to get out of the pool and drip across to answer it with everyone looking. Kate looked the other way like she didn't know me.

'Damien!' I saw that it was my kid brother calling me and hissed into the phone, Ed Foster style. 'Whad'ya-want?'

'I'm bored!'

'Damien, do Mom and Dad know you're making this call?'

'Nope.'

'Then put down the phone, or they'll eat you alive.'

As usual he ignored me. 'These cell-phones are cool. I want one for my birthday. Listen, Joey; Fern's seeing the audio . . . aud . . . the ear doctor about her surgery. And Marcie has to sing a song from the album for the president of America.'

'Great, Damien. Now you're telling me great big lies.'

'It's true. Synergie gets to play at a party. The president's gonna be there.'

'Hey!' Maybe it was true. I'd hear all about it when I got back home.

Meanwhile, I was dripping over the towel and

still feeling goofy. I was also noticing a fully-dressed woman coming across the grass towards Amber Foster's space on the lawn. Too much was happening all at once.

'Listen, Damien, I have to go,' I told him. 'I'll call you later . . .'

'Hey, and Michael Weiss escaped from the cop car.' He dropped this into the conversation before I could click off.

'Cut it out, Damien!' My first reaction was disbelief. Man, that kid had a powerful fantasy life.

' 'Strue! I heard it on the TV last night. Didn't you catch the News Channel?'

I explained to him that not everyone lived their lives glued to a TV monitor. 'Give me the details!' I urged. My second reaction was that there was a remote possibility that it might have happened the way he told it. And then what?

'The cops were taking him from the cells in the precinct station to a real jail outside town. Only they got stuck in a traffic jam. Somehow Weiss jumps out of the car and makes a run for it. The cops can't shoot because there are too many other guys sitting around in the traffic.' Damien had the whole thing taped and he was beginning to convince me. 'Weiss runs into a shopping mall and that's the last thing the cops see. They just put out a warning that he escaped.'

It sounded like the action of a desperate man, but then Weiss fitted that bill for sure. Some cop somewhere was gonna lose his badge over this.

Anyway, I ended up thanking Damien for the message and finishing the call.

The woman who had approached Amber was leaning over, helping to pack up the personal stereo and other belongings laid around the lounger. Kate was climbing out of the pool, signalling for me to come with her to grab our clothes from the locker-rooms.

By the time we'd picked up our stuff, Mrs Foster and Amber were through the turnstile and heading for their parked car.

First problem: how were we gonna follow them?

'Let's grab that cab!' Kate said, hailing one which was passing by out on the Silverton Road.

It turned out he wasn't for hire right at the moment we needed him most. Isn't that the story of your life with cab-drivers?

Meanwhile, Amber had slid in beside her mother who had taken the driver's seat of a rusted, beat-up silver Chevrolet. She seemed to stare at Kate and me as the car passed close by at slow speed. But she looked without seeing somehow. Her mother was talking to her as she exited the hot springs car park, and it seemed to me that Amber's ears were as closed as her vision to what was going on around.

And suddenly it struck me that she wasn't a normal kid at all.

'Cab!' Kate cried to a second driver who was easing out of the pool car park with empty spaces on the back seat.

This one stopped and didn't even blink an eyelid when Kate scrambled in and asked him to follow the Chevvy. Like he played cops and robbers on the road out of this small, time-warp place every day of his life.

'Cool it. We know where they live,' I pointed out to Kate. 'Anyhow, this is a one-horse joint, remember.'

The cab-driver didn't react well to my over-loud description of his hick town. He seemed to deliberately slow down and miss a light, allowing Joelene and Amber to take a left around the corner and disappear from sight.

'Great, Carter!' Kate breathed. 'What now?'

'Drive to Twenty-fifth Street,' I told the cabbie. 'Number 77 . . . please!' I had to add this because I could see from his expression in the overhead mirror that he really didn't like me.

I guess he figured that the sooner he got us to our

destination, the quicker he could grab his fare and dump us. Anyhow, from driving like a snail along the wide Silverton dual carriageway, he set off like a maniac up the narrow back streets. Two tyres scorching the tarmac, screeching brakes; the full works. In fact, he got us where we wanted to be long before Joelene had reached home in her rattling Chevvy.

We'd paid our fare, knowing that the whole street had heard us arrive. Still, we weren't prepared for the welcome Ed Foster gave us.

The cab doors had no sooner slammed shut and the guy pocketed his lousy dough than the owners of numbers 75 and 77 came lumbering down their driveways.

'What did I tell you, Ed?' the neighbour bawled, loud enough to pull others out on to their porches. She liked as big an audience as possible. 'I said these two kids were acting weird!'

What was so weird about arriving in a cab? Or asking a few casual questions? But she obviously had us down as Satan's children.

'Look at them! No way are they friends of Amber's, like they told me!'

Ed Foster didn't take any convincing. Maybe that was because Amber didn't have friends, it seemed to me now. In any case, he came up real close and mean. 'I don't know who you are,' he began. 'And quite frankly, I don't give a damn. All I want is that you exit outta here before I have to put a fist in one of your faces.'

The guy didn't raise his voice, but his fist was up there threatening to fulfil his promise.

Kate stepped back and I moved in front of her to protect her. A real hero. 'We need to speak with Amber,' I said, looking into his red, blinky eyes.

'See, they don't know her!' Mrs Neighbour cawed. 'If they did, they'd never say a thing like that!'

A thing like what? I didn't get it.

'Beat it!' Mr Foster moved his fist a few inches closer to my face.

I stood firm, sensing that Joelene was turning the street corner like the US cavalry riding to the rescue. Her arrival with Amber was sure to put a stop to all this garbage.

The Chevvy pulled up outside the house and Foster swung his fist.

I'd been wrong about the cavalry part. The guy didn't care who saw him commit an act of violence.

The force of the heavy punch knocked me sideways. It felt like my jaw was broken into several small pieces.

Kate stood stunned by the suddenness of the attack.

My bet is that Foster would've waited for me to fall

then stuck his boot in my ribs if it hadn't been for Joelene's fast reaction.

She was half her husband's size and weight, but she wasn't afraid to step between me and him. 'Ed, get back in the house!' she told him. 'Are you out of your mind?'

'They were snoopin' around, asking questions,' he growled.

I was on my knees, holding my jaw in place. Kate was stooped over me, checking that I still had a face. She dabbed with the edge of her T-shirt at the blood coming out of my nose.

'I know. I saw them at Tamaree Springs.' Mrs Foster was also twice as smart as her stupid husband. She'd spotted us briefly in the car park, and now recognised us as the same kids who'd taken the cab. 'So now there's a law against kids asking questions, is there?'

'About Amber!' he explained through clenched teeth. But I saw that he wasn't about to hit me a second time. His wife would make sure of that.

'So?' Joelene began to bundle the heavyweight back up the drive. Then she turned round to make sure that Amber had followed her out of the car. 'Jesus Christ, Ed, just leave it, and let's get inside!'

The numb sensation following straight on from the punch had been replaced by a throbbing that made me hang my head. I had to take one deep, deep breath.

So it was Kate who eased me out of the way to allow Amber to pass.

The girl passed me in a kind of blur.

It was Kate again who later described the look on Elke's twin's face.

'Like there was no one home,' she told me. 'Empty . . . vacant . . . don't bother to knock.'

And I remembered that same expression in the Chevvy. The one that had told me that Elke's twin wasn't a normal kid after all.

'It's real sad!' Mrs Nosy Neighbour had confided in us once all three Fosters had disappeared inside their house and the street was calm again. This woman couldn't resist opening her big mouth, but she'd made sure to take us around the corner, out of sight. 'A couple like that; they adopt a lovely kid like Amber. They already know that things ain't the way they should be with the girl's brain. What d'you do? You agree to adopt and then you're stuck with it for life!'

I was still bleeding all over the lawn of number 75, but Kate had grabbed at the chance to learn more.

'This thing about her brain,' she'd insisted. 'What *exactly* is wrong with her?'

The woman took pride in using a big medical word in

her answer. 'Autism!' she whispered, rolling her eyes and shaking her head. 'That's what they call it. What it means is, poor Amber has no way of communicating with the outside world. It's like she's locked inside her own little world, and she's never, never gonna find her way out!'

9

Carter didn't look his best.

We were back in our economy motel and I was telling him he needed to see a doctor about his swollen jaw.

'Uh-uh!' he mumbled. Meaning 'No'.

'Maybe it's broken.'

'Uh!' Shaking his head, he showed me that he could move the jaw up and down and left and right. No break in the bones.

'Why not get it X-rayed, just to be sure?' Jeez, I acted like his mother, hovering over him and giving him a hard time.

Carter supported his chin in the palm of one hand, dismissing my suggestion with the other. 'What about Gian?' he said with difficulty, through clenched teeth.

Obviously I was gonna have to do all the talking. 'So what's new?' Joey would say.

'What do we know about autism?' I needed to establish a few facts and raked through memories of science lessons and stuff I'd seen on documentaries.

'First, I don't think they have a cure. Treatment helps though. Second, these autistic kids can be pretty destructive. It's like they're frustrated at not being able to make contact. They've no language, no normal way of showing emotions, so they turn in on themselves and beat themselves up. It can be pretty dangerous for the people around them too.'

Carter listened and nodded. There was a cloudy, helpless expression taking shape in his blue eyes.

'Third thing is, they can be gifted.' I recalled this from a programme I'd watched on a kid who could glance at a building like St Peter's in Rome, turn his back and produce a perfect sketch of every arch and pillar. Brilliant. And there are musicians too. It's their inspired way of letting us know what goes on inside their prison-heads.

We sat on Joey's bed, assessing what little information we could scramble together.

'Problem is, there's no way that an autistic kid like Gian can verify Weiss's story,' I said quietly. 'And if we just fly home to Fortune and dump the news about her twin sister's incurable illness in Elke's lap, what good would it do long-term?'

Major dilemma. Catch 22.

We were getting nowhere, so I went down the

corridor with the ice bucket. Carter needed more ice from the machine to help reduce the swelling on his face.

Outside, it was growing dark. The mountains formed a jagged black horizon and the town lights were beginning to twinkle orange, white and pink.

It was a corridor like any other motel corridor, leading to a minimalist reception area – desk, coffee machine, ice-maker. And because it was called Trail's End, there was a pathetic rope tied like a lasso above the door, and a pair of dusty cowboy boots on a ledge above the desk girl's head.

'Sure is hot,' she said as I stood letting blocks of ice churn into the bucket.

'Yep.'

'Air conditioning ain't too good round here.'

'Nope.' In fact, the ancient machines in the small, stuffy rooms cranked and rattled without producing a breath of cool air, as far as I could tell.

'You here on vacation?' Lorraine, the desk clerk, took my replies (minimalist as the hotel decor) as a friendly overture. She was around my age, with light brown hair tied back from a round, pretty face.

I shook my head and gave her a tired smile to let her know I wasn't in the mood for talking.

'Your guy walk into a door?' Lorraine asked with a smirk. Not unkind, just curious. She must have seen Carter walk into the motel holding on to his jaw.

'No and he's not my guy.' Get that straight.

'Yeah, sorry. Anyhow, I heard Ed Foster smacked him in the face.'

This brought me up short as I turned, prepared to head back to Joey's room with the ice. 'You did?' Wow, was this a small town.

'Billie Jean Dixon at number 75,' Lorraine explained. 'She's been shooting her big mouth off ever since it happened. Me and my folks live right across the street.'

This was growing more interesting by the second. 'You do?' I said, leaning the ice bucket on the desk. 'So you know the Fosters?'

Lorraine shrugged. 'Kinda. They don't socialise much. Joelene's too busy taking care of Amber. Ed Foster's just a guy who slobs around.'

'He doesn't have a job?'

'Nope. He sends Joelene out to work at Tamaree Springs for pocket money. He never even child-minded Amber when she was a little kid; just left it all to Joelene. Anyhow, now they have plenty of dough.'

'They do?' My questions didn't need to be sharper

than this; Lorraine was a talker, like a lot of people in this town.

'Sure. They came into some money. No one knows how exactly. But Ed gave up his job filling cars at a gas station on the Interstate. This would be maybe two years back. Actually, they say the Fosters finally got some kind of payout for adopting Amber. It didn't go through officially, they just made some kind of private deal with the real parents . . .'

By this time my attention was one hundred per cent on Lorraine. We stood face to face across the untidy desk, night closing in but still with the temperature way above eighty, and I didn't even notice the ice in the bucket begin to melt. 'These real parents; do you know who they are?'

'Only the guy. And I don't recall his name. He just shows up and hangs around town for a couple of days every now and then. We all know him. He's a loser.'

'But this is Amber's father?'

Lorraine got a buzz out of sharing secrets and rumours. Her face was lit up with the excitement of it. 'Yeah. Thin guy with two days' growth on his chin. Always the same beat up brown leather jacket . . .'

'Yeah, I know him!' I cut in fast. So Weiss had handed over Gian but couldn't let her go completely.

He had to return and hang around. I guess it showed that in his own way he cared. 'Why did he let the Fosters adopt Gi – Amber?'

'Like I say, he's a loser. I'm too young to remember, but according to what I hear, his drinking got out of hand when Amber was around five years old. Before that, they'd lived outside town and he'd done what he could for the poor kid. Then they threatened to put him in a clinic and that was when he decided to hand over Amber for her own good. Not that Ed Foster turned out to be a much better deal than her real dad.'

This sounded tough all round. 'Was it the loser who finally scraped together the dough for the Fosters?'

Lorraine shook her head. 'No way. We reckon that must have been the mother, but no one can say for sure.'

The real mother. Annika. Making a big payout for Gian's upkeep. *Click-click-click*; I punched new buttons on my mental keypad and came up with a surprising image on-screen. It seemed to flash 'Blackmail' at me in a highlighted box.

I needed to be getting back to Joey, to share this and find out his views. 'Great, thanks,' I told Lorraine breathlessly, slopping the melted ice over the edge of the bucket as I grabbed it and head for the corridor.

'Pity about Amber,' the desk girl murmured with genuine sympathy. 'We all hate to see her messed up the way she is. But if you try talking to her, she looks right through you. Always has. Drugs keep her quiet and easy to care for, but they don't give any answers.'

'Yeah, it's terrible.' *Please let me go now! I need another brain working on this!*

'And she's real beautiful when you stop and look at her. I mean, she could've been in the movies . . . anything!'

Or a supermodel. Weird how people stare truth in the face without recognising it. That includes all of us. So don't be surprised that nobody until now had linked up the face on the catwalk with the crazy girl hidden away in downtown Durango. 'I gotta go!' I gasped.

Lorraine watched me set off at a run. 'Hey!' she called in blissful ignorance. 'Your ice has melted!'

Slop-slop over the sides of the bucket. Wet T-shirt, water dripping against my legs. 'Yeah, I know!' I yelled over my shoulder. 'Just hold it. I'll be right back!'

10

Say Ed Foster had put the screws on Annika Svennivig, like Kate said.

My throbbing jaw wasn't letting me think too clearly, but through the fog of pain, I did work out the following.

Go right back to the start. Happy families. Annika and Michael are the proud parents of beautiful twin baby girls. One baby feeds and sleeps, no problem. The other is the baby from hell. Crying, never sleeping, not learning to sit up and do whatever it is babies do.

The doctors do tests. They tell Michael and Annika that Gian has been born with this incurable autism condition.

A thing like that can blow a family apart.

Annika looks strong on the surface, but deep down she's scared she can't cope. She panics and tells Michael that if he wants to keep the kid, it's up to him. But she washes her hands.

I know, it takes a pretty disturbed kind of person to do this, but who knows enough about Annika to say it isn't true?

So the family splits. Michael brings baby Gian to Colorado and keeps quiet about the whole history of the twins, the marriage break-up and everything. He does his best for the kid. But he has a drink problem, and this eventually brings him down.

Then there's the bit about the unofficial adoption – I guess Weiss thought it was the best way for him to keep in touch with his girl. Maybe the adoption agencies had warned him that no way would any father with his history of alcohol abuse be permitted future access to his daughter. That would drive him to make the crazy deal with the Fosters.

'I feel sorry for Weiss,' Kate insisted.

It was gone midnight. So far she'd been back to the ice machine three times, and still I knew the pain in my jaw would keep me awake all night. I'd mumbled to Kate that I thought I'd better take a walk to clear my head, and she'd decided to come with me. We were currently walking along the side of the Animas River, taking in the stars and the crescent moon.

'I know he's a loser,' she continued, 'but he does seem to be the only one in this mess besides Elke who comes out of it with any basic human decency.'

'Maybe Joelene Foster,' I mumbled. It hurt to talk. But I could picture her routine of taking care of an adopted autistic child – a whole lot of feeding, clothing and cleaning up mess that no one ever thanked her for.

'Do you think she's in on the blackmail?'

I shrugged. In my own mind, as we took a bend in the river, heading north out of town, I worked out the turn of the screw part of the story.

Say the Fosters take care of Gian, now renamed Amber. They squeeze whatever money they can out of Weiss for her upkeep, depending on his level of success with Alcoholics Anonymous and his ability to hold down a job. No wonder the poor guy wears the same jacket all his life. He doesn't have much, but what he has he hands over to Ed Foster.

This goes on through the years, and it's not what you'd call real blackmail. But Amber grows up and everyone says how beautiful she is, and doesn't it suck that she is as she is?

Thousands of miles away, a girl called Elke makes it big in the fashion world. She's The Face of the Millennium. Someone – Mrs Stick-your-nose-in-Dixon at number 75 – comes out with the fact that poor Amber bears a striking resemblance to the latest hot property in modelling.

That's when it hits Ed that maybe he's sitting on a goldmine. Suppose he knew enough of Michael Weiss's story to realise there'd been a twin. Weiss had let this much slip during one of his alcoholic binges. Sure, Foster's a lousy slob without too much between the ears. But enough to start putting two and two together and to make his little piggy eyes begin to blink with greed.

'Lorraine said that Ed Foster came into some money about two years back,' Kate said quietly. I could tell we were thinking along parallel lines. 'Say he linked up Amber with Elke at about that time, when she was first appearing in all the magazines. He took a long shot, knowing full well that Amber had a twin somewhere, because Weiss had once let this fact slip. He found he'd hit the bullseye and threatened to blow the whole thing apart unless Annika paid him plenty to keep quiet.'

'Hm.' The nod was enough to show Kate that I'd reached the same conclusion.

Annika thinks she's about to be exposed as the worst parent since Caligula or one of those Roman guys who ate their own kids for breakfast. It would mean scandal, and most likely the ruin of one very brilliant modelling career. Or so Annika might fear.

Yeah, she was one scared lady. She would pay up.

'But that was only the beginning,' Kate went on quietly. We seemed to be drifting towards the empty railway track and following it in the direction of Twenty-fifth Street, as if being on the spot would help us think more clearly. 'Annika makes one payment, then another. Ed Foster keeps on coming back for more. Which is one reason why he was so mad when we showed up asking questions earlier today. A blackmailer is always on edge, waiting to be rumbled.'

To me it also explained why Annika refused to admit any part of the Michael Weiss story, why she kept up with the lie that Elke had never had a twin sister. The more pressure Weiss put on her to come clean and break free of Foster's greedy deal, the louder she told him no. That's just the kind of person she is. It makes Weiss go behind her back to try to talk to Elke directly. And it ends up with Annika fighting her ex and taking a fall down the stairs.

The stars are so far away and faint it makes you feel small.

I'd stopped at the end of Twenty-fifth Street to stare up at them and wonder what the hell to do next.

So the fact that Kate grabbed hold of me and bundled me down behind the nearest parked car took me by surprise and made me think for a second that my luck had finally turned.

'Don't move!' she hissed.

I couldn't. She was practically sitting on top of me.

'Look!'

123

'What am I looking for?' I tried to ask. My jaw was so swollen it felt like speaking through a thick wad of gum.

'In that car parked outside the Fosters' house; there's a guy sitting watching.'

Peering around the edge of the fender, I counted around six cars and trucks parked at the kerbside between us and number 77. Then, in a rented Ford saloon with a Fortune City registration plate, I did see a hunched figure – back view, head and shoulders only.

'It's the middle of the night!' Kate stated the obvious. 'What's he playing at?'

It was a male figure, and OK, it was a suspicious thing to be doing, sitting outside someone's house in the dark for who knew how long.

'Could it be Weiss?' Kate asked.

My heart thumped. 'I guess.'

The guy had escaped and he must be desperate. This was where he'd told Kate and me to come when they'd arrested him. So it figured this was where he would head for too, as soon as he broke free. Only we couldn't see enough of him from this angle and in the dark to be sure.

And we didn't have long to work it out.

The guy in the car must have thought it through and decided to step out on to the sidewalk.

'It is!' Kate breathed. She was still clutching my arm as

Weiss headed up the Fosters' drive.

So we moved slowly along the street after him, feeling weird about stalking a guy in this quiet neighbourhood. I mean, it's one thing on the mean city streets, but it doesn't feel right on an avenue lined with smooth lawns and Hansel and Gretel type houses.

But I guess a person can commit an act of violence here as well as anywhere.

Kate and I reached the house as Joelene Foster answered the door. We saw her recognise Weiss with the same kind of heart-stopping shock that I'd experienced, then watched her try to slam the door in his face.

Weiss had his foot in the way. She stepped out on to the porch and spoke a few words at him, begging him to leave while he still could, before Ed Foster lumbered into the door frame. All three were too busy to notice me and Kate on the dark sidewalk and Amber, who stood like a ghost in a white nightshirt on the stairs behind them.

'Enough, OK!' Weiss yelled. He didn't care who he woke up now that he'd made up his mind to act. 'Foster, you stop all this, you hear me! Annika won't come across with another cent. She's in hospital, for Christ's sake!'

'We watch the News,' Ed Foster replied, low and nasty. He held a phone in his meaty fist and punched numbers into the keypad. 'Do I send for the cops to come and pick you up, or do you beat it out of here?'

Raised voices, bodies shoving each other, feet in the door. Amber stepped down into the hallway in her bare feet, her long hair shining golden in the yellow overhead lamp.

Weiss lunged past Foster, who was strong but slow because of his weight. Knowing that a serious blackmailer was in no position to call in the police, he made it as far as the girl.

'Gian's coming back to Fortune with me!' he yelled, pushing Joelene Foster to one side. 'I say *enough*, before somebody ends up dead!'

The girl tried to pull her wrist free. Her face was empty as outer space.

'It's the only way!' Michael Weiss pleaded. 'If I take you back, Annika will have to admit that you exist. Elke will believe me. We can give you a new start!'

He might as well have saved his breath.

Gian twisted away from Weiss and broke free. Joelene grabbed Weiss. Foster reached up to a cupboard on the wall and pulled out a gun.

Kate and I did the only thing we could think of at this point, which was to move in and let them know what we'd seen and heard.

No way did we figure that Ed Foster would use the

gun. We thought he'd produced it just to frighten Weiss.

But a man hangs on to his ride down easy street. If Weiss took the girl back, Foster would end up serving gas eight 'til seven, day in, day out. Like the rest of us.

'Back off!' he snarled at Kate and me. He twitched the broad nose of the gun towards us and warned us not to set foot through the door.

Hard to take the fat guy seriously in his blue towelling bath-robe and bare legs, minus his glasses, his black hair flopping over his forehead. But the gun was tragic.

Having made sure we knew the score, he swung the barrel back towards Weiss, who had shaken little Joelene off a second time. Weiss now stood with his back to Foster, about to try and reason again with a girl who didn't even recognise her own father.

'I said, back off!' Foster repeated. He clicked off the safety catch on the gun.

We saw Weiss freeze at the tiny metallic sound. Beyond his shoulder, Gian was standing with her head tilted to one side, staring right at the gun.

To aim at Weiss, Foster had to turn his broad back to Kate and me. Did we dare move in on him? Could he pull the trigger faster than we could reach him? Neither of us was prepared to take the risk.

Slowly Michael Weiss turned. Disgust with Foster was

written all over his face. And a kind of recklessness. What did he care if Foster pulled the trigger? The cops wanted him for attempted homicide. His whole life had fallen apart.

So he walked right up to Foster, whose gun shook in his hand, past him as far as Kate and me standing out on the porch. 'Give me an answer!' he pleaded. 'Tell me what to do!'

'We can sort it out,' Kate whispered slowly, as if a loud, quick noise would frighten Foster and make him pull the trigger. 'We'll back you. They'll have to believe us!'

Maybe it was this promise that made Foster do it. Later, Kate was convinced that she was the one who finally signed Weiss's death warrant. It made her hard to console.

Anyhow, Foster squeezed the trigger and fired. He shot Michael Weiss in the back at point blank range.

The guy spun with the force of the explosion ripping through his body. He faced his daughter, took one last look, then his eyes glazed and he sank to the floor.

Joelene screamed and Gian shot forward like a puppet on a string. She flung herself down on the ground on top of the body, wrapping her arms around it, covering her white nightshirt and her golden hair, her beautiful face in blood.

I wouldn't swear on the Bible, but for a second I thought she knew what had happened.

A door opened. But she couldn't bear what she saw, so she went back inside her dark room.

11

Someone was gonna end up dead, like Michael Weiss said. And it turned out to be him.

It felt like my fault.

No way should I have given Michael the answer I did: 'We can work it out.' It scared Foster into pulling the trigger. I should've faked it, said, 'C'mon, let's get out of here. There's no way you can win.'

Then, when there was no gun pointing at his back, Weiss could've come to the cops with us and told them the whole story.

Life is full of 'ifs', but this is always gonna be one of my biggest.

Carter was sweet, said it wasn't down to me.

It was late Thursday, and we were on a plane back to Fortune City.

'We' meaning Carter, me, a nurse, a social worker and Gian.

Rewind.

Weiss was dead in a pool of blood, Gian went on crying loud and as if forever.

Joelene froze in a corner of the hallway, while Ed Foster stared at the gun in his hand. The guy had no clear intention in his mind when he pulled the trigger; you could see amazement on his face. It was the same when he threw a punch at Joey – something snapped and he lost control.

Of course, much earlier than this, Billie Jean Dixon had called the cops. She couldn't let a major disturbance in the neighbourhood go by without interfering.

So they arrived maybe two minutes too late. Not early enough to stop Foster the psychopath shooting Weiss, but in time to prevent him and Joelene getting their act together and getting the hell out of there.

(Apportioning sympathy as well as blame. I do think all this is hard on Joelene. Sure, she never stopped her husband from blackmailing Annika, but the woman had done the best she could for Gian for more than ten years. Anyhow, I wouldn't send her to jail for what she *didn't* do. The judge might, though. There'll be a trial. Joelene faces charges of being an accessory to blackmail and homicide.)

And how come Carter and me are sitting on a plane

with Gian less than twenty-four hours later?

The medics moved in fast. They cleaned her up and calmed her down with drugs. Autistic kids hate to deal with change, the doctor told us. They keep objects in the same order – felt tip pens along a table, each colour with its exact place in the row.

Blow their world apart, like Foster did for Gian, and you get a big mess to clear up.

They established next of kin via me and Carter. We told the cops, the medics and the social workers the whole story. Joelene had the decency to admit everything.

That made Annika lying in her hospital bed Gian's closest family member, and Elke on her way back from Tokyo. So they drugged Gian up to the eyeballs and brought her home on the plane with us.

The poor kid sat in total isolation. 'Extreme autistic aloneness'. That's the official term. Carter read a textbook about it during the flight.

No response in her eyes. Oblivious to where she was. Prolonged inactivity was a symptom of the disorder, the male nurse, Kiefer, explained. Like; no movement, not a flicker of expression on that mask-like face.

In Gian's case there was mutism (no speech), plus a

preoccupation with mechanical objects. For instance, in the room in the Durango clinic where she received treatment, she would turn the light switch on and off for hours on end. Plus, Gian displayed an insensitivity to pain. She could cut or burn herself by accident and never even react. Luckily, Kiefer said, she wasn't deliberately self-destructive.

The plan was to transfer her to a clinic in Fortune City. This had been Elke's idea when they contacted her in Japan. 'Bring her home,' was what she said.

Annika was informed.

She went into major collapse – needed sedation, cried a lot, admitted too late that she'd made up the whole story about Weiss trying to kill her.

She'll need long-term therapy, they say.

Apart from anything else, facing up to what she'd done to Gian and Elke when they were babies was gonna take a whole lot of work.

But anyway, Fortune City Hospital was the place where we all headed on Friday morning.

To everyone's surprise, Annika had made the first move by asking to see Gian. Elke said she would come straight from the airport to join them. She was also very clear that she wanted me and Joey to be there too.

Which was weird for us. But nothing compared with what Annika went through the first time she set eyes on Gian.

That happened before Elke arrived, due to a delay in Immigration.

They'd taken Annika out of the body brace and allowed her to sit up in bed in her private room. I thought she looked more together than I would've expected, after what they'd told us. Her eyes were a little puffy; there was none of that force of personality that had been her trademark. But she was calm when Gian walked in.

Kiefer sat the girl down beside the bed. You saw the resemblance between mother and daughter, but no interaction.

Gian stared at the monitors behind the bed. She liked mechanical objects, remember.

At first Annika hardly dared look at Gian. *This is the daughter I abandoned, denied, erased. This is my guilt.*

I glanced at Carter. He gave a small, almost invisible shrug. ('You want to know the biggest irony?' he said later. 'Gian's so sick that she doesn't even know what her mother did to her. Annika's going through all that guilty conscience stuff for nothing.')

The silent reunion seemed to go on forever. Feelings darting around the room without ever meeting their target. I was hating it, until Annika finally reached out her hand and touched Gian's cheek.

Not much, but a beginning.

Elke finally arrived when Kiefer and the medical staff had settled Gian into the psychiatric clinic which was in the same building as the Accident and Emergency unit.

Carter and I went to meet her in Reception, to bring her along to Gian's room.

'What do we tell her?' Carter asked as our shoes squeaked down the shiny corridor.

'We say, don't expect too much.' I for one wasn't looking forward to the look on Elke's face when she met her twin sister for the first time.

'. . . It's OK.' Elke greeted us quietly. 'I'm not falling apart. In a way, this is too big. You don't lose it over the really huge things.'

'I'm sorry about your father,' Carter said, up-front.

Elke nodded. She closed her eyes for a second and put her hand up to her face. A deep breath, then she was back in control.

'I was thinking about my mother,' she confessed as

we walked her back along the corridor. 'What she's been through.'

Which was pretty damn big of her. I mean, I guess parents can act real badly. They can do stuff that you'd think would turn their kids against them. You'd expect a kid like Elke to hate a mother like Annika. But she didn't.

I got the feeling from Elke that she wouldn't be pushed around by Annika any more. But that she'd never give up on her the way Annika had given up on Gian.

So there was this beautiful girl walking into a hospital room to meet her twin.

Carter and I stayed at the door.

Gian had her coloured pens arranged across her table. She had her back to Elke, head down, blonde hair falling forward. She was drawing the scene from the hospital window: walls, fire-escapes, three pigeons sitting on a wire.

Eventually she heard a noise and turned to face Elke. It must have been like looking into a mirror. Except for the eyes.

Deep down she must have recognised her.

And when Elke put her hand into her pocket and drew out a small plastic envelope, I cried.

Inside the envelope were the two twists of hair. Elke took them out and showed them to Gian.

Gian noticed. She liked their softness, their golden shininess. So she took them from Elke and stroked them against her face.

TREATMENT

Early infantile autism is a label coined by Kanner in 1943. Literal meaning, 'selfism'.

There's a question about whether the condition is inborn or acquired during the first three years of life.

I found that it was rare. Only one per 5,000 kids are affected. More boys than girls.

There are various suggested treatments, but none is completely effective.

I read a lot about it because I needed to understand.

If I can get my head around stuff, it stops my feelings from taking control.

Like Kate, I could've cried.

Treatment includes the use of neuroleptic drugs such as haloperidol and serotonin-reducing ones like fenfluramine. These can be disappointing and they include side effects.

Yeah, they mess with an already messed up brain. Sure there are side effects.

The specialist in Fortune City put Gian on dietary therapy, reducing her intake of carbohydrates and boosting Vitamin B6 with regular pills. Dr Swanson believes that this alternative is worth a try. It's something new for Gian and she may respond.

Otherwise, it's the old behavioural approach, plus a bit of cognitive stuff – don't worry about it. It means they increase the amount of appropriate stimulation to try and bring the autistic patient out of their own little world. For Gian, they plan to develop a programme of sign language to help her communicate.

I was telling all this stuff to Connie, Zig and Zoey, once it was all over and we were back to normal, in my basement, playing Synergie's new track.

'The bottom line is, we're all alone,' Zig said.

We all stared.

He amazed us a second time by blushing and carrying on. 'An autistic kid is just more alone than the rest of us.'

Zig's not just a pretty face who can throw a ball into a basket after all.

Zoey looked disappointed; not the kind of stuff you want your boyfriend to come out with.

I glanced at Kate for her reaction.

'Yeah,' she sighed. 'I guess.'

There was a long pause.

So that was how she felt. When it comes down to it, we're all in a state of extreme aloneness.

'But . . .' Kate broke the silence. She meant to be kind to Zoey, but I have hopes that she aimed the remark at me too – 'that's where love comes in. When we break down the barriers and make contact. When we find the one person in this world who has a snowball in hell's chance of understanding who we are!'